Isidore

By the same author

Fiction
Inhabiting Shadows

Non-Fiction
Madness – The Price of Poetry
Lipstick, Sex and Poetry (autobiography)

Poetry
Nineties

JEREMY REED

Isidore

A novel about the Comte de Lautréamont

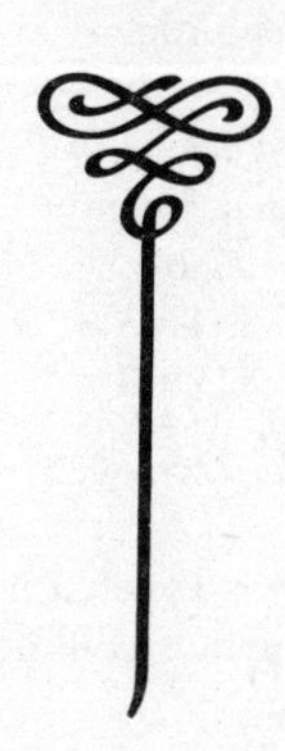

PETER OWEN
LONDON & CHESTER SPRINGS PA

PETER OWEN PUBLISHERS
73 Kenway Road London SW5 0RE
Peter Owen books are distributed in the USA by
Dufour Editions Inc. Chester Springs PA 19425–0449

First published in Great Britain 1991

British Library Cataloguing in Publication Data
Reed, Jeremy
Isidore.
I. Title
823.914

ISBN 0–7206–0831–7

Typesetting by Action Typesetting of Gloucester
Printed in Great Britain by Billings of Worcester

For Rolf Vasellari

Flaubert said to us today: 'The story, the plot of a novel is of no interest to me. When I write a novel I aim at rendering a colour, a shade. For instance, in my Carthaginian novel, I want to do something purple. The rest, the characters and the plot, is a mere detail. In *Madame Bovary*, all I wanted to do was to render a grey colour, the mouldy colour of a wood-louse's existence. The story of the novel mattered so little to me that a few days before starting on it I still had in mind a very different Madame Bovary from the one I created: the setting and the overall tone were the same, but she was to have been a chaste and devout old maid. And then I realised that she would have been an impossible character.'

The Goncourt Journals, 17th March 1861

Contents

(*on facing page*)

Etching by Salvador Dali for the fine limited edition of *Les Chants de Maldoror* by Isidore Ducasse, Comte de Lautréamont, published by Skira in 1934. (Reproduced from W.J. Strachan, *The Artist and the Book in France*, Peter Owen, London, 1969)

Does Anyone Know?
An Interview with Isidore Ducasse, Comte de Lautréamont

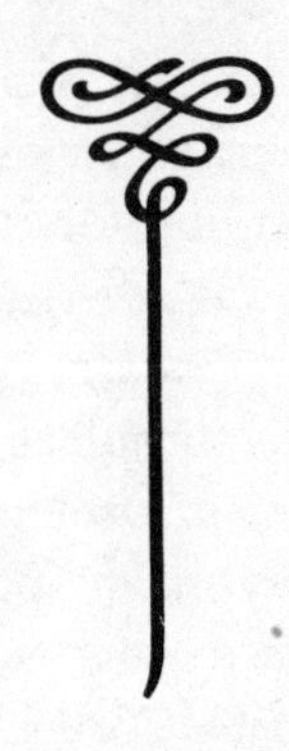

The interview takes place in the Sahara. White table and white chairs. A white canopy is spread over the speakers.

Interviewer: You lived to see *Les Chants de Maldoror* published in a complete edition by Lacroix, Verboeckhoven, Brussels, in 1869. Censorship problems prevented the book from becoming known, and for almost half a century it remained an underground classic. Why was it that your book disappeared for so long?

Lautréamont: At the time, there were hints of reviving the Tribunal de la Seine. It was impossible to publish in the latter days of the Second Empire without risking prosecution for obscenity. The book as I remember received a brief advertisement in Evariste Carrance's anthology *Fleurs et fruits*, and a note in the monthly *Bulletin du bibliophile et du bibliothécaire*, and that was it.

Interviewer: When the surrealists placed you alongside Baudelaire and Rimbaud as one of the poetic revolutionaries whose work belonged to the twentieth rather than the nineteenth century, were you surprised?

Lautréamont: I was out in the desert by then. That's my code word for the state in which I now find myself. Without realising it I suppose I liberated the stream of consciousness. I hit upon a detonative period. The old novel with its formalised plot was dead. Poetry with its inherited classicism was drained of all meaning. Without really trying for it, I aimed for something wild. I wanted a simultaneous reversion to primitivism and an imagery that was distinctly modern.

Interviewer: You lived in turbulent times. I suppose you're unwilling to speak about your formative years in Montevideo, and the ones leading up to your disappearance in 1870?

Lautréamont: In a letter to my publisher Verboeckhoven, which you assure me was dated 23rd October 1868, I outlined a belief that has come to be much quoted. I referred to *Maldoror* as 'the beginning of a publication which will only be completed later, after my death. Thus the moral of the end has not yet been drawn'. We weren't so very far away from the Commune and the siege of Paris by the Prussian Army. I was writing against the opposition asserted by my death, although I was convinced that the latter would come about in response to an inner dictate, and not as a consequence of revolution. I had already conceived the idea that my work would be taken up by a new generation and completed through the cataclysmic upheavals of a more violent century.

Interviewer: I suppose you were too close to your work to realise its full significance. What I wonder would have happened had you known that Rimbaud was sixteen at the time of your disappearance, and had already written some of the most powerful visionary poems of his brief life? I still hold to the theory that he had read *Maldoror* before composing his own valediction to poetry – *Une saison en enfer*. How else explain the self-deprecatory pyrotechnics, the hallucinated vision that seems to stem from your seminal work?

Lautréamont: Perhaps that's why we meet in the desert. But no, what happened was that we both located the subliminal unconscious at a time when no one else realised its potential. Rimbaud and I meet now, but at the time we were unknown to each other. He broke away to the desert in flight from a vision that threatened him with madness. Perhaps I was more detached. I channelled my delirium into my writing. It has been suggested by critics that I was mad, that I spent my Paris years in a madhouse. That I ate paper and wrote in blood on the walls of a cell. Evaluating my past, as much as we ever can do in the light of experience, I think there were other more controlled facets to my character.

Interviewer: I'm interested in the intention behind your work. André Breton describes *Maldoror* as 'the expression of a total revelation which seems to surpass human capacities', and Henry Miller writes of you that 'His predecessor was Jonathan Swift and his chief executor was the Marquis de Sade'. These seem to me to be statements that leave you as an abstraction. They serve only to increase the idea of a person who may never have existed.

Lautréamont: I'm not sure that I ever wrote for an audience. I remember connecting with a current that was so huge it impressed on me my isolation. Originally *Maldoror* contained specific references to Georges Dazet, a former school-friend, but I deleted these. There seemed little point in clinging to human reference. Implosions are a part of psychic spontaneity. The correspondence I found between an umbrella and a sewing-machine, for instance, opened up the way for a new manner of sighting metaphor.

Interviewer: You wrote in your *Poésies* that 'To struggle against evil is to accord it too much honour.' There's a sense in everything you wrote of someone who saw too clearly to be constrained by a time or a place. Was literature then an accident? Could you as easily have become an arms dealer like Rimbaud?

Lautréamont: I can only answer this question in part. It seems that poetry because of its peculiar synthesising properties picks up on external events through recourse to subjective crises. But then Rimbaud had a specific death. I was simply nominated Death Certificate no. 2028 signed by a hotel proprietor and a member of his staff. The question is left open in your mind as to whether I was temporarily buried in the Cimetière du Nord or lived on in another capacity. And if I did, would that person be any the less real than the one you confront now?

Interviewer: Again, if I may quote a modern reading of your work, André Breton claims that *Maldoror* is 'the very manifesto of convulsive poetry'. We have grown almost by association to think of you as connected with a movement in literature that was to occur half a century after *Maldoror* was conceived. And perhaps the biographical confusion stems from here. A full life in terms of years would have seen you live into the first decades of the twentieth century.

Lautréamont: I suppose your question leads directly to the interpretation of literature. There is in every epoch what we call an ideological tension. My childhood in South America was distinguished by political insurrection. Something of that must have contributed to the sadistic atrocities in *Maldoror*. How else can one explain the abnormal deviations in my work? Copulation with a shark, the crab that enters my anus, God's visit to a brothel, infanticides, murders, a pack laying into a transsexual in a wood. That would be one reading. But I'm careful to make clear that *Maldoror* inhabits 'the dark recesses and secret fibres of consciousness'. There is now a more distinct vocabulary for describing inner states, but I was concerned not so much with Poe's metaphysical hells as with mental images. A continuous psychic explosion. I had already found the tone of disgust that I relished in Baudelaire, but I wanted to push language to breaking-point and to explore the sexual fantasies which might have become pathological if they weren't cycled by the imagination into a poetic context.

Interviewer: The dark glasses and white suit you have adopted for this interview enforce the almost predictable ambiguity that has come to surround your person. I spoke of Rimbaud earlier in connection with your work, but in this century your 'convulsive' imagination seems to have been inherited by Jean Genet. His early novels share your preoccupation with extravagant ritual as well as embracing sexual fantasies which are correspondingly mutilative. Would you comment on this?

Lautréamont: It's natural that the outsider, the man in flight from himself, the sexual and social outlaw should inherit something of my preoccupations. Or what were mine. You must remember that I have acquired other dimensions since that brief intense period during which I wrote *Maldoror*. It was a time of unrealised strain. In finding a new mode of expression I intersected with what were to be the characteristics of a new age. Universal war and the discovery of the psyche. But I'd lived through that on an inner plane. Unresolvable moral issues still rage within the pages of my book.

Interviewer: What little we know about your life has come down to us largely through the sketchy recollections of your school-friend, Paul Lespès. He didn't give us his portrait of you until he was eighty-one, so there may be reasons to doubt its accuracy. He mentions your long hair, shrill voice, intransigent nature, the extravagant imagery that characterised your schoolboy poetry. But the myth surrounding your madness is enforced by statements like 'above all, his groundless fits of bad temper, in short all his strangeness, made us feel that he was somewhat unbalanced'. He mentions also a speech you gave at school, 'La folle du logis', which, according to Lespès, 'piled up a frightening plethora of the most horrible images of death. It was nothing but broken bones, hanging guts, bleeding or pulped flesh'. Would you say that these statements contain at least a partial truth?

Lautréamont: I have to be careful here. There's the myth attached to the writing and the one attached to the person. How do we ever differentiate between them? Reality is transformed by the imagination into fiction. Words are fictions – they alter how we see or experience the world. And because their function is the business of the poet, he either chooses to become their product – that is, mythicises himself – or else clearly distinguishes between the work and his person. My experience is that the two are inseparable. Sadism interested me in terms of the book I was writing, therefore it may have been a part of my person.

Interviewer: How much of one's life does one remember?

Lautréamont: Not that much when we're living it. Then it appears like a film, only it's speeded up, and we imagine that it is life which is directing the camera independent of us, and not we who are responsible for consciousness. My life was divided roughly into two halves. My childhood years in Montevideo and the years spent at Tarbes and later in Paris. My childhood was a solitary one spent in French colonial South America, but the natural beauty of the place, combined with a sense of not really belonging, helped to create the solitary vision I was to bring to *Maldoror*.

Interviewer: When a work like *Maldoror*, which so radically alters the shift of consciousness, appears, the silence with which it is greeted by the Establishment invariably means that the vision expressed awaits discovery. You were particularly fortunate to find in André Breton so eloquent and revolutionary a spokesman. Is it chance, accident or design which has placed *Maldoror* in the mainstream of European literature?

Lautréamont: This desert light is painful. I'm still not used to it even after a century. To get back to your question, though, I suppose in the heat of writing *Maldoror* I didn't care about the book's future. You have reminded me that I wrote of my intentions: 'It is not right that everyone should read the pages which follow; only a few will be able to relish this bitter fruit with impunity.' Youthful admonition or a truth? Those who took up my thread had realised in themselves its continuity through their work. Isn't that always the way?

Interviewer: In *Maldoror* you confess to crimes that we can either take literally or interpret within the context of the violence generated by the work. How are we to read this claim: 'I even murdered (not long ago!) a pederast who was not responding adequately to my passion; I threw his body down a disused well, and there is no decisive evidence against me.'

Lautréamont: The question is too personal. We've already proposed that in the absence of a biography the work lives in the place of the author.

Interviewer: It interests me as to how you originally conceived the form that *Maldoror* was to take. It is only late in the book that you express your belief in the affirmative power of the novel, by which time the book has acquired its own fragmentary narration.

Lautréamont: Anything that starts out with the intention of being a novel is a lie. The imagination works contrary to the arbitrary impositions of character and plot. I went with the stream of consciousness. When I saw that certain threads remained consistent, I pulled a noose before letting my subject drop.

Interviewer: You end *Maldoror* on the image of a hanged man, a policy of mutilation begun almost at the book's outset when the protagonist slashes his mouth with a penknife. For we the readers it's convenient to link the self-destructiveness manifested in your work with your early death. But for you the process must have been quite different. How would you describe the relationship between the two?

Lautréamont: There isn't one. A century in the desert has convinced me that the attempt to construct a life – that is to say, what you have tried to do in your novel – is simply one fiction elaborating another.

Interviewer: And in the end?

Lautréamont: Does anyone know?

Two empty white chairs face a white sun. A car driven off at high speed raises a dust-cloud.

Part One

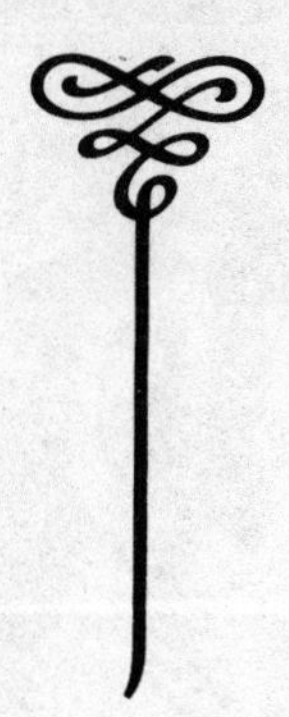

Woodcut of Lautréamont by Adolfo Pastor, after the daguerreotype
by Armand Vasseur

The Eye 1

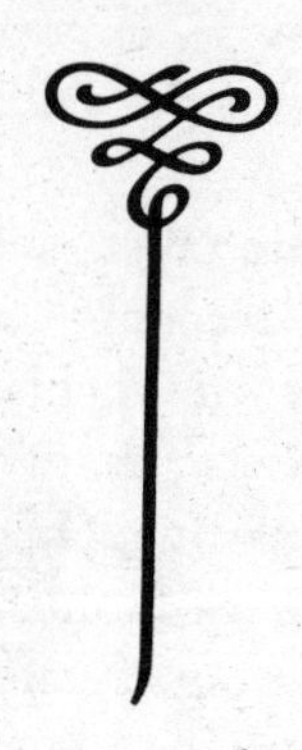

Subject: Isidore Ducasse. Born 9 a.m., 4th April 1846. Place of birth: Calle Camacua, Montevideo. Father: François Ducasse (b. 1809), Deputy Secretary, French Consulate; Mother: Célestine-Jacquette Davezac (b. 1821), deceased.
16th November 1847: Isidore-Lucien Ducasse christened at the Metropolitan Church of the Immaculate Conception, Montevideo. Education: Private tutor – Gustave Flammarion, bachelor (?).

Notes compiled for François Ducasse

I have begun to follow your son with increasing regularity. The boy's solitary nature confirms your anxiety about his being too much alone. I have noticed that he treats his tutor with a disdain uncommon in one so young and thinks nothing of riding into town when he should be attending a tutorial. It would appear indiscreet of me to suggest that Monsieur Flammarion, far from taking disciplinary action, seems to be a complicitous or consenting party to your son's truancy. You ask me for facts and I present them. I cannot pursue that avenue of inquiry without your permission. Gustave Flammarion may or may not be responsible for your son's early failings, but he has a part in them.

The books that your son takes such pains to conceal are by authors that you will recognise as inflammatory to the imagination. Byron's *Manfred*, Mickiewicz's *Konrad Wallenrod*, Baudelaire's *Les Fleurs du mal*, the works of Poe and the more conventional likes of Lamartine, Hugo and Alfred de Musset.

On two occasions last week I followed Isidore Ducasse to the town centre. He has a favourite café in Independence Square called El Sol Negro, where he sits alone drinking coffee and observing Montevideo's cosmopolitanism. He rarely speaks to strangers, his purpose being to watch.

In fact it is the degree of his inaction which fascinates. On two separate occasions he has been approached by men and held in conversation for longish periods. His natural shyness dissipates at such times. These types are usually foreigners, single, resident at the American or Imperial Hotel.

You ask that I spare you nothing in my confidential reports, and I venture to suggest without conclusive proof that your son is attracted to members of his own sex. For a young man he expresses little interest in women. He has to this date shown no interest in the town's brothels and formed no friendships. He is always alone, whether it is in the town, riding without permission in the countryside or sitting knees up, meditating for hours on a deserted beach.

It is from watching your son's solitary hours on the shore that I have come to establish another tenuous connection which I hope in time to develop. He is himself being constantly watched by a figure concealed in the cliffside grasses. I can gain no lead on this man. His occupation may be better known to your department. His involvement has something to do with ships –

a wrecker, a smuggler, a trafficker in contraband? His binoculars are regularly trained on your son's activity, which seems to be nothing more than that of someone who wishes to be alone by the sea.

I am certain that both characters are unknown to each other. I shall designate this man as X in future communications.

Long observation tells me that your son walks with a stoop, though I cannot say if it is *affected* or natural. He is also liable in moments of elation to develop a limp in the left leg as though comically imitating a character study. These outbreaks are further evidence of his undisciplined nature.

I hope to be able to build on my preliminary investigations and provide you with more detailed accounts. Flammarion's private notes on your son read:

Possibly a classicist but lacks discipline. Decadent leanings that find a resonance in my own area of experience. Too solitary to learn from the discourse of others. Excitable imagination. Fascination with bestiaries, the antediluvian world of monsters. Could be put to purposeful use in my cause if it weren't for an unrelenting obstinacy. I suspect he knows the truth about his parents?

Chapter 1

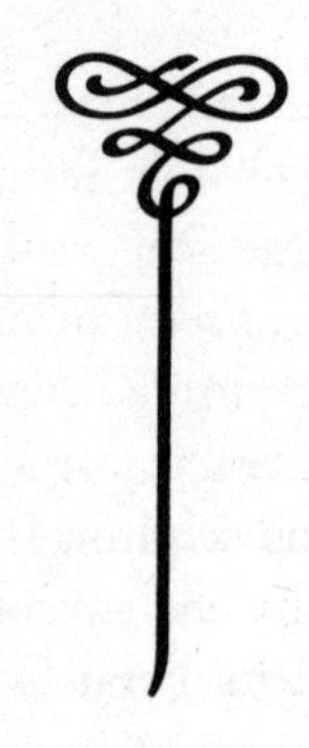

It was the clock by which I lived, persistent and without duration, the measured flood of surf involving my ear like a shell caught up in the undertow. I could hear it in the lapses between fever, the universal rhythm of tides, the world rolled like a pearl through emerald gulleys. Sometimes the wind would report on a wreck breaking up on a reef, its hull dislodged and dragged over a coral steeple. I would imagine its sunken cabins sequined by luminous shoals of fish, their collective motion resembling aquatic butterflies.

On my bedside table were the shells I had dived for or filched from a cove. It was their completion that fascinated me. Nothing was left to chance. Their colouring was dictated by their habitat, and correspondingly brought to mind the multicoloured pockets of the sea, its brilliant fauna, vermilion and yellow prairies of weed, fronds vibrating in the current.

A diver showed me how to extract the mollusc from the shell

with a corkscrew twist of the knife, but more often I buried my trophy in the sand and allowed the ants to clean the interior. When I heard my father pejoratively snapping my name, I would place my ear to the rose-coloured helix and listen to the roar inside my head. That way I was alone again, basking on a ledge, my mind given up to the sun and the wave unrolling a white hem of lace on the sand.

When my father's voice intruded on my silence, I grew confused. His inquiry had the effect of a stitch coming undone in the seamless fabric I called my inner dialogue. He was stiff, imperious, inflexible in his dictates. I would watch him pacing the balcony, and I knew by the pauses in his metronomic beat when he was thinking of her, and how the image of her face must have arrested his mechanical step. His rigidity disguised an almost imperceptible limp which would develop in times of crisis. He must have lived with the refusal to recognise its autonomy ever since he had come to live in Uruguay, and had renounced his small teaching post in a village in the Hautes-Pyrénées. He kept a watch on it – the slightest hint of any physical defect and he would have lost face. It was only my diligent watching that discovered it, and tonight his secret was pronounced. His left leg spasmodically twitched without his seeking to redress the action.

I could see the sequins of sweat oiling his forehead, his head comically pepperpot-squat on a Roman neck, his white linen torso corseted by a red sash. His felt hat rested on a white cane chair, together with an open copy of Balzac that would be meticulously returned to its library shelf in the morning. It must have been something more than his life as a teacher that inclined him to amass so curious a collection of books. I never tired of poring over the plates of natural curiosities, monsters said to be extinct. There were huge armour-plated dinosaurs, cumbersome mastodons and great ground-sloths uprooting a tree bodily. The primitive bestiaries came alive at night. I learnt to people my dream landscapes by prolonged meditation on pictorial images.

If I closed my eyes I could trap the monster in my head, afford it life in the great inner spaces where nothing has ever died or relinquished its right to terrorise. I declared war on the dark gods, their horned buffalo heads and red eyes watched me from wooded summits. I was granted a cheetah's speed, I could never be taken captive – a gold wind-arrow pursuing a flight arc that took in a plain at a single stride.

Solitary, at odds with colonialism, I paced the beaches anticipating an encounter that would convince me of the meaning of reality. I watched fishermen put out at dawn on a serene sea, a white sail on the horizon pricking up like a cat's ear in response to wind. I saw gold coins flung back in an officer's face by a half-dressed girl, tinkling as they rained down on stones.

When my father threatened that next year I would be sent away to board at the Lycée Impérial of Tarbes, I allowed his words to escape me. I made believe that by ignoring the directive, Father would in time forget. His manner of addressing me was so unreservedly formal that he gave the appearance of standing back from his words, as though absolving himself from the inconsequence of speaking to a minor. He seemed frightened that language implied a moral responsibility, a psychological evaluation of the manner in which we express our thoughts. He was irritable, peremptory, his moustache stained with coffee, and I backed out of his study into the green sunlight, then took off at a run behind our house, making for the bay with its long, dazzling surf-line, the sapphire water disclosing a ribbed sea-floor of zebra stripes, a nervous cloud of pink fish taking off into deeper water.

I was resolved to stow away, to punish my father for his indifference and create a scandal amongst the colonial community. Obscenities, recriminations, telescopic metaphors crowded my head. I took out my notebook and began penning my anger by way of release. All of the frustration evolved over years of restraint flooded out of me like the deadly black ink of a cuttlefish.

My dear Father

By the time you receive this letter I shall be on the high seas bound for Bordeaux. You will nonchalantly draw on a cigar, assess your diminishing assets and delight in the attraction presented by your new sense of a bachelor's freedom. They will never know, as I do, the truth of what happened to Mother, and how she must forever rise as a drowned body in the black pool of your unconscious. You forget that I was there that day on the beach.

As one whose vocation is to be a poet, I thought I would entertain you with an allegory from my stock of inherited madness.

– There was this man and he took root in his house. He secured himself to it like a clam its shell, and the walls digested his secrets. In the dark of the night he would think I am invisible, people have accepted my station, and he would refer to his library shelves as conspirators in his plot. When he heard of a man who lived in a hut on a vertical cliff, shelved above a dead drop to the sea, he broke out in a cold, vertiginous sweat. The prospect unbalanced him. He began to dream of the place, and his oneiric visions were of himself becoming a bird that lacked the gravity to return to earth. His obsession with the precariousness of this cliff-hut compelled him to visit it.

He set out on a day of sea-mist and rain. A vessel had foundered off the coast that night. It could be seen upended, prow down in the open shark's jaw of a hidden gulley. When he arrived at the coastguard's shack, his repeated knocking on the door met with no response from the person he knew to be inside. He could hear someone moving about the room quite naturally, oblivious to his repeated summons. The rain was blowing off the face of the sea, a white smoke that saturated his military greatcoat. He could hear the man indoors working with a hammer, and to his confused senses it seemed as though the door was being boarded up against his entry. His hand went numb and it was only when it dropped involuntarily to his side that the hammering stopped. Simultaneous with the abrupt reintroduction of silence he noticed big flowering-currant sprays of blood on the thin, white timbers, and the rawness of his knuckles stung where the skin had shredded.

He stood there a long time staring at his damaged fist, the skin peeled open like the corolla of a lily. The wind had risen, threatening his own safety, and he charged inland, head down and butting through the grasses. He expected at any moment to hear the foundations give and the house plummet over the cliff into an angry head of white water. Several times his imagination audibly created the sound, but it was only the renewed assault of waves detonating at the cliff base. He pushed through tall streamers of grass, his coat teeming with ducts of rain, the panic mounting in him as he tore deeper into unknown territory.

When he got back to the town, he remembered his rank and adopted a martial strut – eyes fixed on the skyline, back erect. To his astonishment a great crowd was milling on the outskirts of his residence. The animated buzz resembled that of a disturbed hornets' nest. He pushed his way through their disorder and found that his house had been levelled by the tempest. Nothing stood upright. The roof had been pitched into a nearby plantation, the walls slatted, and incongruously only his heavy oak desk remained anchored to the site. When he moved closer, something shifted with the wind, layers of pink chiffon bordered with pearls and fluted with salmon lace had him think of a wounded bird, a flamingo trying to lift from the grasses. It was only when he prodded it with the ferrule of his cane that he recognised it as one of his wife's petticoats. He stood back and watched it soar birdlike with the gust and spiral up high into the underface of a sooty cloud, a migrant off-course and lashed by the storm. It hung motionless for a second and then disappeared in a series of rapid loops.

The man buried his damaged fist in the earth of his foundations and traced out these words: *A house of blood is open for all to see, whereas a house of paper withstands the hurricane.*

I left off writing, my nerves pacified by the black venom-trail of my pen. I realised how little I spoke of psychological issues, how rarely I committed my inner world to speech. Instead I recorded it in words, huddled over my notebook like a man crouched in front of a fire, the ink-blotches showing like berry stains. I had to keep these concealed from the inquisitiveness of our maid, Alma, whose shadow mooned over every surface of my room. Her lips pouted whenever she crossed my bedroom mirror, giving one the impression that she had just bitten into a raspberry. Alma was a local girl from the village, a mulatto whose unstudied walk had the rhythmic pitch of a belly-dancer. Her hips completed an imaginary circle with each motion of her body as though her intention was to rotate rather than propel herself forwards.

I would watch that quiver, which seemed to radiate from the base of her spine through the cleft of her bottom, and wonder if the balls of her feet were balanced on oranges. Her language was one of gesture, not speech. She lacked the element of mistrust in natural phenomena that so characterised the tension in our house. My father, for all his reserve and unassailable hauteur, was terrified by the outbreak of storm. If an electric storm broke over the gulf at night, I would hear him go downstairs and unstopper a decanter. Then the pacing would begin, a drawer would be opened and shut, papers would crackle with the urgency of fire rushing through brushwood. This disturbance would last for the duration of the thunder – the anxiety of a caged jaguar, its beat constricted by the confines of its cage. In the morning the purple rim left by the discolouration of

Father's monocle would be outlined like a bruise. The air would smoulder with the reek of cigars, and the orderly quiet of the study admit to the rampage that had ransacked cupboard and drawer in the early hours of magenta light shot with quicksilver.

Alma went about the house like a somnambulist. What she did not wish to see, she bypassed. Her thin dress acquired the line of her body, and on rainy days one could imagine the tight, mauve buds of her nipples flowering from expansive breasts. It was not desire I experienced so much as a confused apprehension to witness my opposite. I had believed that the self was an inexhaustible study, a beach that one could never cross owing to the complexity of ciphers scored in the sand. One was a long time in kneeling to examine each new cryptogram that evolved from a sensory awakening. The triangular imprint left by the oyster-catcher was slashed and crossed by a graph sheet of conflicting signs. One could spend a lifetime searching out the oyster-catcher's trail to the exclusion of any other alternative. There was no end to the maze, and all that summer I felt an increasing dissatisfaction with my inability to enter into the tidal current of other lives. No sooner had I raised my horns from the involuted turban of my shell, than I retracted. The big events happened inside; it was there I could establish my province.

I got into the habit of making nocturnal excursions to the shore. Lights flickered from small fishing-craft rounding the coast. The lighthouse was a moving arc against the stars. When I closed my eyes, the seascape was contained within me like a ship inside a bottle. If you kept on doing that, I told myself, you became God. Once you had achieved the internalisation of the universe, your proportionate expansion demanded a cosmic awareness. In that way the mystic eye could see the universe as a child's clear blue marble – a crystal sphere balanced on a projecting ray of light.

The beach was my imaginary kingdom. I imagined myself as a sea-king, solitary, listening to the beat of surf, my head on my knees at the edge of the world. Everything existed only because of my consciousness. I was the seed that germinated in the void, and already I knew Baudelaire's *Les Fleurs du mal*, the works of Mickiewicz, Byron, Musset and the psychological hells devised by Poe. I saw myself as the child in Baudelaire's *Le Voyage* who sits with his maps and stamps by lamplight, only my precocity allowed not so much for amazement at the vastness of the universe as boredom when I realised that its discovery would afford only a sense of the predictable. I had already lived the poem's trajectory and suffered its conclusion: 'Beyond the known world to seek out the new.'

If I sat absorbed by my own reflection, it was because I believed that the magnification of the particular comprised our only access to knowledge.

My father would be away for days at a time. He would be gone at the head of a small diplomatic party, his features set into an impersonal mask, and only the thin sickle-blade of his mouth, the upper lip hidden by a sandy moustache, revealed the inhumanity he translated into a devotion to duty. There were uprisings everywhere, insurrectionist blacks firing the houses of Europeans, squalling through flame for the pickings of loot – chamber-pots, jewel-caskets, gowns of Bordeaux-blue velvet which in time would become sweat drenched and slashed in a cane thicket.

I would sit on a chair in the portico overlooking the courtyard and make up stories, which I pretended to narrate to a figure who stood below me. He was called Hermione. Hermione was the protean form that embodied my chameleonic flights of mood. Alma could not see him. On the one occasion when I mistakenly owned to his identity, she adopted a peremptory manner and suggested I go indoors and lie down with the shutters closed. 'But then he'd only come inside,' I replied. 'We're interchangeable. He might look out of me and you'd never know.'

Sometimes when Father was away for a prolonged period I

would ride into Montevideo and drink coffee in Independence Square. If a boat had put in, there would be the excited milling of crowds, irregular panopticons of trunks lashed to a carriage that rattled towards the Panaderia del Sol.

But even in the comparative serenity of the capital I could sense the uprising that was to come. I could smell the pungent histamine of grass-fires and hear the spar-jarring collapse of rafters. There was the reverberant sound of cattle breaking across country pursued by a red overhanging wave of fire. And the women, even in my juvenile imagination, were being twisted into impossible extravaganzas of geometry – legs somersaulting over their heads, a soldier dancing on the world triangle, forcing his pleasure to the exclusion of time and place, realising through the mounting surf of his climax the momentum that forces a tidal wave over a white cliff-face. The sense of imminent destruction was with me as I stood outside the Duplessis Bank, calle Cerrito, watching the rich plantation holders arrive, their plutocratic diffidence pronounced by their reserve, the conviction that they need never die in a country which offered such continual beneficence. They would be found one day in an outback, a colony living on in orange and lemon groves, the perfumed blossoms snowing their laps, their wisdom as old as stone.

My youth burned with precocity. Standing still in the middle of the square in Montevideo, I would feel myself levitate, lifted by a big wind that seemed to displace me from the limitations of the present and establish me in a century I should never live to see. The consciousness of being at odds with my age also extended to a dislike of my body. Tall, thin, slightly stooped, my raffish blond hair curtaining my forehead, I was awkward, odd as a heron as I stood still listening to my thoughts well up from a subterranean cavern. The shrillness of my voice was an oddity like Shelley's. Day after day I would see it, his blackened skull picked out of the roaring pyre on the beach, bone scoured by the fire, Byron spitting into the ashes, cursing the green sky, stubbing his club-foot on a charred timber, subduing the impulse to smash the triumphant death's head on a cauldron of rocks. I could smell the red hecatomb, the black wick of smoke swathing into the azure sky. Shelley with his violet eyes had dispersed into the elements he had celebrated. His small mourning party walked back up the beach, elated, still unable to equate death with the sanded drags of smoke, the blue dazzle of light above the sea.

Hermione wouldn't go away in times like these. He was just there, waiting between me and the light as a sign that the narrative was to begin. He would surprise me on the portico while I cradled my glass of lime sorbet and listened to a woodpecker drilling up high in a tree-top. Or he would intrude at dinner. I would stop in mid-sentence, tumble over the cohesion of my words, drop a knife or fork, to the outraged rancour of my father, who would redden, but I was overtaken, lifted out of the present and transported into fragments of a fiction. I was witness to two sailors' brawling in an alley over a red-haired woman who lifted her skirt higher and higher as an enticement to the one who should win. When the scene changed, I was the solitary figure waiting on the beach in a blue boating cloak for the news that would come of the birth of a king in the islands. The child was guarded in a black marble villa by two sisters sworn to keep the secret of his parentage. Already he wrote in his own blood as a mark of his absolute authority. He would drape the mirrors, for if he were to see himself, it meant death. He would prepare speeches for his eventual voyage to Rome, and in his mind hear the voluminous approbation of the stadiums. He would die by night in Venice, rowed in a gondola across black, star-lit canals, the potency of a swallowed aphrodisiac raging in his poisoned entrails, the masked figure lying beside him on cushions, already forcing the rings off his fingers. 'Noli-me-tangere. Suck my cock.'

I would be ordered from the table. My father would stand up, his cheeks turned claret, and watch me leave in a silent rage. It was at such moments I would observe the buried youth in him. I would see the sapling inside the gnarled features of the weathered tree. Without the moustache trained into the shape of a circumflex accent, and the discoloured eye-rings of the insomniac, his figure relieved of the ballast accumulated at diplomatic dining-tables, it was possible to see a young man stooping to blue gentians on a mountain-slope, excited by the anticipation of what life might come to reveal. I would stare at a candle-flame as the tension drew tight like a bowstring. A lilac oval quivered inside the orange halo. That light was responsible for the illusory pentimento of Father's youth.

I continued to stare at him in the way a sculptor cuts the waste marble free of the intrinsic form he has preconceived. I kept on wishing he could see himself as the candle allowed me to imagine him: a young man leading the girl who was my mother across a field of tempestuous anemones, their petals resembling a rainbow arched over a magenta wash. Father had lost thirty years in standing up. I wanted him to remain like this, a figure created by flame, hollowed and dabbed by gold and blue.

I was to be punished for day-dreaming; my father couldn't tolerate unresponsiveness to his politically informed conversation. There was news of Louis-Napoleon's expansive liberalism, of a Paris liberated from the despotism of Louis-Philippe's Second Republic – women waking to find diamonds under their satin pillows, the gunfire of champagne corks, dukes pissing into chamber-pots in the small hours, *Vox Populi, vox Dei!* inscribed on the blue-black night sky above Notre-Dame.

I was ordered to bed by an implacable silence. Outside my window I could hear the tireless susurration of surf, the Atlantic expiring in a white ruff on the moonlit beach. And beyond that horizon? I was already there. The world would offer me a straw with which to negotiate the labyrinth – I could see my shadow huge in a corridor, drunk on the reek of animal, following through to the hurricane contained in the bull's eye.

The Eye 2

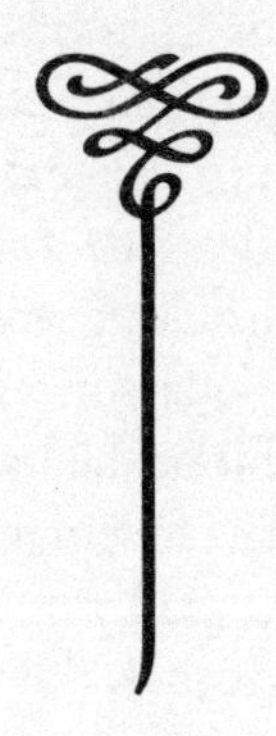

Recurrent lapses in tutorial attendance. I wonder that this aspect of your son's behaviour is not made apparent to you through Monsieur Flammarion.

Of a more disturbing nature is the boy's attraction to scenes of violence, something that was first drawn to my attention by a stable-hand. The horse ridden by Isidore has several times been returned with vicious welts cut into its flanks by the use of a whip and spurs. If he rides for an afternoon, a horse is ruined for a week.

On the 5th, 8th, 12th, 23rd and 27th of this month your son visited the capital. I had expected his visits to be motivated by the need for stimulus or devised with the intention of making brief contact with strangers in town. Your son is careful to avoid acquaintance with residents of Montevideo. In this respect his instincts are remarkably advanced for a young man. His judgement is infallible. He responds to the one approach that he knows is safe.

On the 12th and 23rd events took a more serious turn. I observed Isidore Ducasse leave the Imperial Hotel and walk diagonally across the town. His direction took him towards the abattoir situated on the outskirts of the poor quarter. On the 12th he was chased off from the site by a gaucho, but returned an hour later and managed to conceal himself behind offal-bins in the yard. I need not describe for you the butchery that characterises this place. Shrieking animals are brought to the ground and slaughtered. Your son appeared unmoved by the sight of such unrelenting bloodshed and returned again on the 23rd. This time he bribed the foreman and was allowed to enter the abattoir. The workers paid no attention to his presence, despite the neatness of his clothes, the oddness of his being there. His intense absorption, the stiff movements of his body, seem to suggest a compulsion that is close to trance.

Blood-stained clothes. Took his shirt to the beach, washed and dried it in the heat.

Three days at home engaged in writing and close study. On the 27th he set out for town about an hour before noon. Intense heat and an atmosphere of unrest that characterises the carnival preparations. I followed Isidore Ducasse to Independence Square, where he deposited a letter at the American Hotel. He then made his way towards the central market, an unsafe area which I understand he is forbidden to visit. Fireworks were already being released from the roof-tops.

In one of the filth-littered streets behind the market your son was challenged by a masked figure, dressed for the carnival, who effectively cut off your son's right of way by occupying a position in the middle of the road.

Something about this man, his light stature, his movements, has me associate him with X, whom I have referred to in my previous report.

The police report will have filled you in with details of the incident.

Suspect: Ruben Machado
Occupation: Unknown
Address: 3 Bista del Mar
Other Relevant Information: Former sailor, speaks French and English. Known to the police. No convictions in Montevideo.

Chapter 2

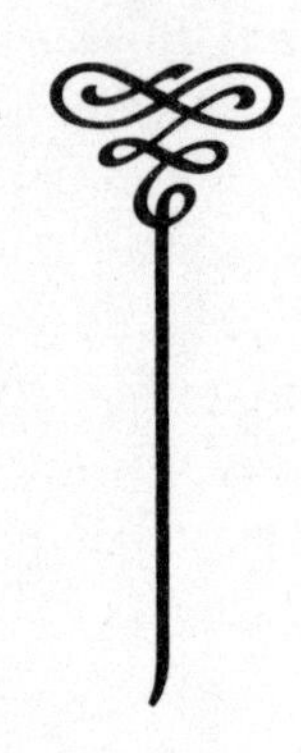

When the last of the panic-stricken animals had entered the abattoir, the gaucho, pursued by his attendants, galloped outside the enclosure round to the other side of the yard. There he dismounted and retrieved from the ground a long, thick rope manufactured from raw skin, and tied it to his saddle-ring. In the course of watching I realised that that leather rope was a flexible lasso, the loop of which was slung over a pulley. The man standing inside the yard brandished it several times above his head, before his aim directed itself round a bullock's horns. Simultaneous with the lasso finding its target, the horseman spurred his animal to a quick uptake, and by means of this opposition brought the captive bullock to the ground, dragging him at the same time close to the spot where the man who had thrown the lasso was waiting with his knife to dispatch the animal close behind the horns.

The first time I witnessed this I felt compelled to go on

watching, despite the trapped herd's stampede, the contained hysteria of horses, the ferocity of the killing. The dead animal was then dropped through a trapdoor on to a truck that ran along the sheds on iron rails. Six men waited at the terminus to lift the carcass from the carriage and begin immediately to skin and dress it. The procedure went on for hours with monotonous regularity. Somehow, although I had never wished to encounter such scenes of brutality, and by now my white shirt was flecked with a fine spray of blood carried on the wind, I was mesmerised by the subversion of my own heroic myth in which I ventured my life against a single intractable force that stood between me and the blue sea-roads leading to the future.

On several occasions I surprised myself on the way to the abattoir. I would start as though caught in the act of theft, and pull up short on the road. I could not decide whether it was I or another who hurried with such intent towards the scene of slaughter. I expected to find myself sitting in my room, the windows flung open on the day, dreaming the incident, so that at a switch of my thoughts the action could be erased – the projected double hauled back in on a lifeline.

I stood back against the whitewashed wall of a courtyard and breathed in the scent of aloes. It was I who was standing there using up unrepeatable moments of a life that appeared to have fallen like a coin on its rim so that both sides were visible alternatives, one depicting the sharply relieved circle of an oroborus, the other a caduceus. That thin circle of gold caught fire in the sunlight. I imagined it dropped by someone hurrying to catch the ferry to the underworld.

I was journeying towards blood in streets already hectic with preparation for the three-day carnival. There was a simmer of gunpowder in the dry pre-carnival air. Someone had paint-splashed the name Juan Manuel de Rosas on the wall of a suspected agitator's house. His dictatorship had ended when I was a child of six, but people still spat whenever his name was mentioned. Tomorrow fire-balloons would drift out over the harbour with its imposing lighthouse. Masked orgiasts would patrol the streets; women with a silver tassel on each nipple and faces sequined with cosmetics would stream through the alleys leading to the Customs House and the Hotel Oriental. All day the mask-makers would be at work, elaborating on papier-mâché grotesques, clowns' faces, primitive warrior expressions, and somewhere a death's head, a lantern-jawed, white skull staring out of the dark at a braying donkey.

I hurried on; the air smelt of saltpetre from the fireworks that had been prematurely released into the daylight sky. Orange and black, they had gone up as a flight of orioles before exploding into pyrotechnical blossoms of a blue flame-tree.

I should have been at home reading Racine or Corneille for my private tutorials aimed at preparing me for the lycée at Tarbes. Flammarion was an old Bonapartist who had fled to Montevideo under the France of the Citizen-King Louis-Philippe, and talked constantly of returning to Louis-Napoleon's Paris. He was a small, understated individual who seemed forever about to impart an intimate secret to an imaginary audience. His etiquette was as polished as the silver tip of his walking-cane. He carried a top hat and wore the check suits made popular by the Comte de Walewski. I distrusted this asthmatic, punctilious man and his anecdotal memory, the watery glaze in his grey eyes that seemed to hint at the existence of collateral bands of thought, a forked tongue that undermined his façade of sincerity. And there were the hours when he was to be heard talking to Father in his study. It was a different voice I heard then, the inflexions being more variable, the intonations more volubly masculine. It could not be me they were discussing at such length, although in the black thunder of my mood I imagined I was the exhibit in a glass dome on show between the two of them. Were they conniving to be rid of me, or was the pedantic Monsieur Flammarion impressing Father with his intimate knowledge of the colour scheme of the Empress's apartments at the Tuileries? What was it that fascinated him about the portrait of the Prince Imperial as a child, wearing the broad red ribbon of the Légion d'honneur on his little white frock-coat? Details, punctums, the illusory never separated from the real.

I could hear delirious laughter coming from the open window of a villa. Someone was throwing water-bombs in the street, pelting me, and I felt their cold, detonating shock. I was struck on the left shoulder and then the crown of the head, to the accompaniment of the dull report of a firework flourishing an emerald mare's tail in the blue sky. I pressed on through streets reeking of a filth that was in contradiction to the cosmopolitan innovations of our city, its architectural parallelograms, its sea air smelling of jasmine and mimosa. A harlequin darted out of a doorway dressed in a spangled jacket, yellow tights and a pink face-mask. I pulled up short, challenged by this confrontation in a side-street, the figure barring my way, moving with a boxer's feint to left and right, disguising his intentions under a clown's red-painted mouth. I backed off and he advanced; I went forward and he retreated. A spider's tacky thread had contrived to join us – an invisible but tightly binding line linked our umbilicals, drawing us now forward and now back on a wavering tension cord. When I looked round, the alley was blocked behind me by a crowd that had gathered, sealing off my exit to the thoroughfare. Simultaneously a group of masked figures had gathered behind my unknown antagonist. They stood with their backs to the wall, pretending indifference but all the while vitally alert to our every movement. Without my being conscious of it, the distance had narrowed between us, and for the first time I could see the black drill-holes of eyes in the slit apertures of the cerise mask. The figure facing me was deceptively misproportioned, the shoulders padded inside the tight-fitting scarlet jacket, the hair scraped up beneath a tricorn and tied in a bow, a white froth of lace concealing the chest. The jacket flashed a rain-storm of brilliants.

I stood fixed in the white, sunlit street. I was ice in the

noonday heat; resolute in my determination to cut my way through the crowd. I was experiencing the same excitement as on the first time I was allowed to ride without instruction. The division between my own momentum and that of the effortless rhythm of the horse beneath me had so vanished that I neglected to take in the overworked steaming flanks, the hot fleck of saliva, the repeated incision of my spurs. On my return I was thrashed by the groom, but I was drunk on speed, intoxicated by the huge spaces I had swallowed. I still seemed to hang over a green furnace of grasslands, a figure autonomously projected into an overreach of the future. Thereafter I should always be a fraction ahead of myself.

Again the figure closed. I kept wondering what had caused our lives to intermesh, and if the figure were not in some way connected with the abattoir, and my hanging around there when the fat cattle were driven into their waiting pens.

I could see the handle of a knife resting partly concealed on the outside of my opponent's right leg. The tension was exacting. A fly punched across my vision on a squib-fuse. I could feel the crowd willing the conflict as an incitement to the riotous festival that would begin at nightfall.

I was forbidden to be here, that was what drummed in my head; fear of my father and not that of my antagonist interposed as the only division between me and my opponent. I was to be constrained to the prospect of festive fire-balloons floating across the bay, from the roof-top. Blood, salt, ammonia. I could smell them in the air, the pungent ingredients that predicted physical conflict. We narrowed again, close enough this time for me to see false breasts in my antagonist's shirt. I had the feeling that he somehow knew more about me than I did myself; he had acquired an extra dimension on me that I had still to find in my psychological make-up. He was at an advantage, his features concealed and distorted, deflecting me away from the identity that showed through his eyes.

People had gathered on the adjacent roof-tops, nonchalant,

indifferent, immune to the outcome of another knife fight, but interested enough to keep half an eye on us.

I was too light for my opponent, my schoolboy's body would be thrown or kicked at the first interlocking of bodies. I was half the man's weight, armed with a small boating-knife although he did not know it, a foreigner in the mixed Spanish and Italian neighbourhood. Involuntarily I was devising a strategy, mapping out my hit-points, my possible avenues of escape. The rush was beginning to occur in me, I could feel the adrenalin forcing my blood, I had to restrain myself from making the first improvident move.

A solid backdrop looked on, a tableau depicting the curious, the accidental and those whose natural impulse quickened the undercurrent of impending violence. Time in its concentration seemed indefinitely extended. I was both here in this alley and elsewhere, and it was my vision of somewhere else that told me I was not going to die. I envisaged myself years on, a slim young man in a black velvet coat, foxed at the elbows, looking out of an attic window at sun-burnished spires. In order to get there I had to eliminate my opponent. The cord uniting us grew more assertive in its vibrancy. The dust irritated my nostrils, worked through to the lining of my throat, and settled there. Then the blaze occurred, a whiplash of lightning had me veer wide of my opponent's triggered projection, his hand simultaneously finding the knife as he ran through the space I had occupied, my feint sending me chin down in the dust, to the accompaniment of an uproar as the onlookers shrieked, at which the military gendarmerie cut through, lashing to right and left with savage cuts of their horse-whips, dispersing people with indiscriminate brutality. A dismounting officer tore the sequined eye-mask from my opponent to reveal the face of a young woman, her black-eyed Italian features scored by a horizontal scar across her forehead. She was beaten and left on the pavement of a street that did not even own to a shadow. Meanwhile the spectators had deliquesced into the blue vapour of the afternoon. I stood there, the knee of my black breeches torn, the elbow of my shirt shredded.

I was driven home in a landau, silent, white-faced with rage at the indignity of being escorted back to my father's house. We passed orange and banana plantations, and here and there the black shade cast by a fig tree. Some of the European houses had drives bordered by Australian gum trees, and in one an ombu offered a cool and impenetrable penumbra. As we drove along I could recognise the tiru-riru of a thorn-bird, or the firewood gatherer as Alma called it on account of its propensity to collect sticks for building purposes.

I was uncommunicative with the two officers who escorted me home. They doubtless wanted to be free of their charge and to return to the city for the dubious pleasures of the carnival. Restraint was exercised by no faction, and only last year the chief of police had been found drugged, stripped of his uniform and credentials in a bad part of the old city, his body ballooning like a fish in a hammock strung up in a native girl's room. It was in this district I had been found, in an alley behind the principal plaza which had been built by the Spaniards, and divided by a flagway from the chief market at the Plaza de Independencia. My guilt was a private one; neither of these two men could have known that I was on my way to the abattoir to experience the butchery of droves of hysterical cattle. And although I should have to account for my presence in the old quarter, I was still the threatened victim with rights of protection and not the unlawful antagonist.

When we entered the drive, with its hectic azalea flames, I knew from the horse standing there, patient, head bowed, that Monsieur Flammarion must have been waiting for over two hours in the house, impatient to resolve and punish my flagrant breach of courtesy. The question of my safety would not have occurred to him; his concern would be the inconvenience he had suffered.

Alma answered the slightly rolling toll of the doorbell, and while I stormed upstairs without so much as a word of greeting, one of the officers was received by Monsieur Flammarion in the library. I locked my door and remained deaf to Alma's solicitations. I wanted to be alone, and already I had conceived the notion of writing about the experience. Only by doing so could I extract it detail by detail from my head. The transference of the indelibly visual to the medium of words would by that exchange alter the experience, so that both I and the event would become something else in the telling. I wanted to be a part of that change already. I imagined that if I could appear before Monsieur Flammarion as the person embodied in my intended fiction, I should be beyond his reach. There would be a confusion quite different from a lie in how I related the incident. It occurred to me that one could grow to live like this. To anticipate one's actions by their fictional occurrence.

I stood by the window listening for the reassurance of the sea. Its movement was always there even if you could not hear it, its vibration connected with my breathing, the hollowed curve of my diaphragm.

I was interrupted by Monsieur Flammarion's authoritative double-knock. He knew there was no need to speak; his dictates were imperative without ever having to be enforced. I went obediently to the door and opened it. He stood there, his hands behind his back, chest elevated, his expressionless eyes aimed at a point behind my shoulder. He was wearing a bullfinch-pink waistcoat beneath a sober grey suit. He appeared to have been drinking. I could smell juniper on his breath, the almost eau-de-Cologne scent that distinguished gin.

'I should like a word with you downstairs' was all he said before turning on his heel and leaving me no alternative but to follow him.

When I knocked at the door I was admitted to a room full of the Empire furniture and bibelots that my mother had shipped from Europe. The ponderous furniture had the air of knowing it would outlive you. I had the feeling as I faced Monsieur

Flammarion that the nineteenth century would remain weighted down by the ballast of its drawing-rooms, its cardamon-scented studies.

The silence in the room deepened until I could make-believe I was walking underwater, opening my mouth in fish-ovals against a blanketing wall of sea.

'I shan't tire you with the details of a situation of which you are fully aware,' Monsieur Flammarion began, his eyes fixed on one of the two little Italian landscapes. 'You have not only disobeyed your father's instructions that you should keep away from the city during the period of carnival. You have insulted me by missing your tutorial.'

I had already lost interest in the situation and was looking at the light filtering through the aromatic gum leaves outside the window. If I were to be sent away on that interminable Atlantic passage to Bordeaux, it was my wish to go now. I would punish Father subsequently by my incommunicativeness; his letters would demand the obedience it was in my power to withhold. I would leave him nothing, only my mother's face, inaccessible in death, her features resisting any attempt on his part to re-establish their physical likeness to mine. I had already penetrated beyond the express status of individuals to probe the putrefying molluscs in their shells.

'Word of this will reach your father, even if I should refrain out of delicacy from mentioning it,' Monsieur Flammarion was saying, unable to conceal the latent pleasure he took in acting out the role of a duplicitous intermediary. 'Let me tell you,' he continued, 'should you lose your father's trust, your inheritance will be imperilled. You'd do well to view power not as an imposition but as the unifying undercurrent that determines our place in the social hierarchy.'

Monsieur Flammarion polished the little glassy full moon circumscribed by a rain-halo that served as a monocle. His manner had relented; the implacable indignation of his mood had devolved to the reminiscent. I was suspicious of this switch of tactics, the brightening of his eye that I had learnt to read as a barometric register indicating cross-currents.

'These are difficult times,' he continued. 'Something I shall have more to say of in my memoirs. This country has been subject to continual violent revolutions. Out here, men die like pigs.'

There was a silence I punctuated with both real and imaginary surf. I wanted to be out on the coast watching the water brighten from sapphire to kingfisher as it flooded into the shallows.

'If you were a commoner, Ducasse,' Monsieur Flammarion resumed, 'the incident would be of little significance. But given your father's position and the extreme tenuousness of the political situation, your presence in what I understand to be a disreputable quarter requires a careful defence.'

It occurred to me that this piece of subtlety was the line I was being offered to enter into a conspiracy with the insignificant, pedantic man who aspired to state honours. For a long time I had suspected Monsieur Flammarion of going through Father's private papers. My suspicions were founded not on any tangible proof but on an attitude of mind that secretly desired recognition for actions it was forced in the interests of propriety to conceal. His cleverness was in allowing me to observe his silence. The vulnerability, the tensions I learnt to decode in him as a surer sign than language were all clues to a guilt in which I was somehow implicated. His invisible spider's web had been slowly settling on my face. Now he could observe his delicate artistry, the interweaving of his thoughts with my own.

'I am also to inform you', Monsieur Flammarion continued, 'that your father will be away for the period of the carnival on official duty. He has gone to San José, entrusting you to my charge. My advice to you is to go upstairs and make amends for the tutorial you missed this afternoon. I shall then discuss with you over dinner how a compromise can appear so signal a victory as to hold in check a potential that is too ruthless to admit to the field. It is not experience one acquires with age, it is more a knowledge of how best to capitalise on those situations where the strength withheld is assumed superior to the weakness manifested.'

Monsieur Flammarion lapsed into a partial silence; he was seeking my tacit approval by allowing his words to weigh in my mind. They went the way you throw stones in the shallows and watch them plummet in delayed spirals to the sandy bottom. I could pick them out by their mineral patterns – a blue, a green, an ox-blood stone embedded in its own shadow.

When I went upstairs to my room, I was further resolved in my determination to run away. I could feel the tyranny of the mid-nineteenth century tighten an iron cummerbund round my breathing. My father was unapproachable, my mother dead, and now my tutor was attempting to involve me in an illicit complicity against my father. I looked out of the window and felt the blue air beating its cool volutes of flame against my chest. What I saw with unmitigated clarity was not the whitewashed villas holding to the arc of the coast but the opening out of a timeless dimension, a cone of light through which I saw the gathering of peoples, the survivors milling together in a lunar landscape, the sky livid with warheads, a black rainbow arching over all. This visionary landscape had excluded the immediate one. I was realising the transforming power of the imagination and how reality was an inexhaustible lake inside me, a water rising on me. If I were to live, I had to learn to defend that province, to sit and meditate on black lakes like a swan quiet in the smoky reprieve of twilight. I was made suddenly aware that the secret was within me. The red jaguar running across a royal-blue beach under a zebra-striped sky existed because I had conceived it.

I could not concentrate on Racine's *Phèdre*. I thirsted for lines that would burn into my nerves. If it was to Baudelaire and Poe I turned most often for the sustenance of crowding on sail in my anxiety to reach the void, it was to the incredulous sobriety of Montaigne's mind that I switched when seeking support for the unnatural.

Inwardly I fumed. Monsieur Flammarion would have resettled to his book. It would be Chateaubriand's *Mémoires*, but a part of him would not be reading at all, it would be measuring its prey, moving a beam of light over the image it had selected to trap. Somewhere at some moment I had registered as a potential in his scheme, the elevated arrow-head had bristled on my spine, and without my knowing it I had been marked.

Outside, a wind picked at the espaliered fruit-nets and shook the plumed tassels of pampas-grass.

I could hear Alma stop outside the door and hesitate. Her presence was defined by her breathing. I could sense that she was standing on tiptoe; the tension had persuaded her to follow the trajectory of her nerves in their straining towards an unrealised completion. I had to imagine what she was thinking, rooted there, her mind already engaged in perfecting what she had still to achieve. I focused on the page and gave myself up to the automatic writing that I had come to find so pointed a directive to the transcription of the unconscious.

> When I set out on the road for the lost city of Zalziba, I looked through a mirage at a herd of unicorns standing amongst flamingos in a blue pool. A summit stood upside-down in the glare like a thimble-top. I watched its snow-cap crown the waters, measure them like a plummet, and suspend from their heights the primal image, the god in the form of the drowned man, choked like a water-rat in the crystal of his creation.
>
> I continued my journey, and encountered a carriage drawn by four white tigers headed towards a villa lost behind maples.
>
> I stood watching it go, and a young girl, her blouse open on breasts full blown as yellow roses, approached me and handed me a long-stemmed hookah. She had run away from the old scholar I had seen returning to his estate. He had spent a lifetime in the study of the relation between the

tidal currents of the Bosporus and the erotic rhythm of the body at the heightened moments of orgasm. . . .

Alma's light tap on the door found me dissociated. I did not want the muffled drum of her knuckles to intrude on my narrative. Within the limited radius of my life there was nobody in whom I could confide. The adult world seemed to be engaged in a perpetual conspiracy against the young, and to have adopted an inveterate antagonism amongst themselves.

I let her second and third knock go, and when finally I opened the door I recognised the smell of Mother's perfume: ashes of violets refined in Paris and sold in expensive crystal phials. Alma was heavy with it, a displeasing invasion that had me think she was wearing a borrowed skin. Her black eyes looked without seeing at the shambles of my bed, the surf of papers overlapping my desk, the disorder of my senses reflected in the disarray of my room. I wanted to protect my creative chaos, admonish her from the room, but her eyes came at me in ways that were disarming, as though she had discovered in me the pliant strings of a guitar that awaited only the play of her fingertips. This subtilised inner body that had been a source of such conflict to me was being drawn to the surface of my skin. I was both outraged and compelled by the suggestion of her advances, the instructive intensity of her stare forcing me into an apparent role of provocation. I fell back on the bed and continued falling through a well-shaft of unconscious imagery. Fragments of street scenes exploded into life. Soldiers were hustling a young Mexican out of an alley, his mouth still bruised by the juice of a pomegranate. Heat-whitened parallelograms, trapezoids, rhombs broke up the attempt to have a landscape slow down and stabilise. I was watching a fishing-boat sit in a bowl of light off the coast. Then the roar of surf was gaining in my ears: the universe was blacking out as lips folded into and funnelled my breath, their location shifting to leave scorch-marks on my neck and throat. Without any assistance on my part Alma was kneading her breasts against me, swimming in slow motion through planes that shattered like ice on my confused uptake.

I tried to push myself out from under, but the rhythmic spiral of her pelvis had connected with my own excitement. Something embodied in me was turning larval, a fire that I was not sure how properly to direct was gaining, fanning its heat towards an instinctive outlet. As her positioning pivoted on me I began to submit and feel myself cushioned by the tide rather than forced underwater. I was being instructed into that rhythm the way a dancer picks up on the drum tattoo, the clap of maracas. I was being lifted on a wave that gathered in momentum. It had begun to run for the shore, its gradient slanted, tilting, almost sheer in its concave arc, fetching me up in its overhang, compelling me forward in the white dazzle of its fomenting roar, the savage thunder of its detonation.

Then she was gone. I lay there soaked in a hollow of the bed, the phosphorus burning inside my skull. Now that it was over I had to convince myself of the reality of what had happened.

The house was still silent. Somewhere in its cavernous interior Monsieur Flammarion must have fallen asleep over his book. Our very separate apprehension of the world at this moment in time impressed on me the isolation in which each individual lives.

I lay back and allowed the flood of physical warmth to suffuse me. Swallows were diving in the air outside, skimming the eaves in the frenetic zigzag of their aerial chase, with whiplash elasticity. If I prolonged the moment indefinitely I could go on living it. The wave would become a frieze, a timeless transparency in which the afternoon would depict Monsieur Flammarion asleep over a calf-bound book, the stages by which Alma advanced to seduce me, Father's carriage frozen in its journey to San José, swallows cutting a wing-dip above the sea – and over it all, flushing the marble pink, the invisible and transforming rays of my mind.

The Eye 3

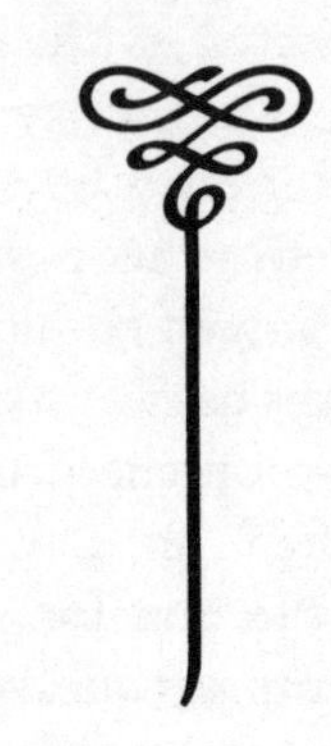

Your absence on official duty coincided with the carnival. From examining the family accounts I see your son lives on an independent income. He likes money – it is part of his superiority in town. But its purchasing power is not used locally. The books he values are brought to him from Paris, and so too are the silk cravats he delights in wearing. He has quickly established a network of contacts. You may wish me to pursue this, but X is the key to breaking the system.

Your housekeeper Alma excites my curiosity, not out of any express interest on my part in her life, but in her relationship to your son and Gustave Flammarion. I naturally find myself asking this question: What does she know that I don't? She is on the inside, and yet the language problem seems insurmountable. I can find no access to her. Does Flammarion? And if he does, then his connection with her involves your son. I trust you follow me. It is my belief that Flammarion has shaped your son's life more than that of his initial acquaintances in Montevideo.

It is extraordinary that one so young can have already decided on preferences in life that seem to owe little to his environmental upbringing. He has already cultivated a love of Chopin and Liszt, attending piano recitals in the home of an American, James Lowell. Whatever he does carries with it the conviction not of a beginner but of someone who is right and whom others in the course of time will follow. What I had taken at first to be a pretentious arrogance I now detect as a form of modest conviction.

On the chief night of the carnival, your son having been upbraided by Monsieur Flammarion and doubtless sent to his room in view of his daytime activities, I saw no purpose in maintaining a watch.

I decided to go into town and stay close to X's house in Bista del Mar. It seemed obvious to me that if your son were to break bounds, he would be found in that district.

Chapter 3

When I awoke it was to find the house silent and a smoky blue dusk flooding the window. I could hear the report of fireworks, the luminous sky blaze of a casa, sky fountains of ruby and emerald ascending in curved parabolas to earth themselves in a rain of cinders. From my window I could see the harbour lit up by the early-evening festivities. There were Portuguese and French three-masters in port, and a billowing wick of gunpowder smoke hung over the town.

I stood at the window breathing in the warm air blown off the Atlantic, trapping it in my shirt folds, my nerves thrumming in anticipation of the carnival I intended to visit in the small hours. The confrontation I had experienced in the morning had left me with the restless desire to seek out my antagonist and, if necessary, renew the challenge asserted earlier in the day. My intuitive faculties told me that my intention was reciprocated, and that somewhere in an alley a transvestite was applying pink snowballs of rouge to a cosmetic mask as a preliminary to the wished-for encounter.

As I stood looking out over the bay it was my mother's face that was suddenly pointed up in my memory. I saw her as she used to look when she visited me in the evenings, her chin dusted with powder, her sea-grey eyes communicating to me from a sense of hurt. If she came to me late, she would untie her hair from a simple black ribbon and pins and let its gold, streaming curls flood her face and shoulders. She spoke to me always as the friend she would have become, had time permitted the establishment of that bond. Even now when I say her name, Célestine-Jacquette, I am conscious of how little she could communicate her sufferings. I was aware of no arguments or altercations between my parents, no visible or audible show of displeasure, and yet the tragic consequences of this ill-suited marriage cannot have been a thing of the moment but rather the corollary to bitter rites – the unspoken language of a cold marriage bed. When Mother visited me in the evenings, she was permitted to re-express her childhood. The simplicity of her early life showed in the manner in which she entered into my love of picture-books and the sailing-ships depicted on stamps, but foremost in the conspiratorial manner in which she narrated our stories, surprising herself as much as me in the way the fiction overtook us, conveyed us as strangers into an unknown territory and threatened to leave us there. We would be alone then, the two of us stranded on a sun-fired island, our boat burning on the sands, our location inaccessible.

The narrative isolated us from Father. He would be downstairs preparing a report, his shadow forming a penumbra over the page, his specious industry guarded with a watchdog's truculence. Mother gave the impression of wishing to stay with me for hours; it was a different world up here with the blue bay visible from the window, and steam- and sailing-ships putting into harbour with their regatta of multicoloured flags. The barriers between us would grow porous and then fluid, and our easy intimacy meet like the confluence of two streams which braid together in a mountain pass before finally resuming their own separate tributaries.

If Mother stayed too long, we would anticipate Alma's subdued knock at the door; and then I would watch her eyes cloud, and the anxiety show in her features the way a breeze places a sudden tremolo in still water. With great ingenuity she would step to the mirror, tie up her hair without Alma's assistance and straighten her skirts as though she had been discovered in the act of visiting a lover. When she turned to go, she had aged ten years and was no longer my conspirator in negotiating islands but a woman obedient to her marital duties.

I dressed for dinner in a white linen suit and white shirt, the collar tied with a black velvet bow. Dressing was simply another ritualised expression of my isolation. I was no more wanted here in this house than I was in a Europeanised town resembling Constantinople on the Atlantic coast of South America. I was unfailingly conscious of the edge; the coast marked a boundary line beyond which everything was abstraction. Somewhere, indefinably lost on my mental map, was the France that my parents had left, and to which by reason of language I would be sent for my education. I was already thirteen, and this afternoon I had experienced my first taste of manhood. Salt and a tingling orgasmic flash.

As a stimulus to the night I could hear a medley of drums, tambourines, piccolos, guitars and cavaquinhos instate the mamba rhythm for a King Momo whose obese, clownish image had already been released in the form of a fire-balloon.

I entered the dining-room to find Monsieur Flammarion already seated at the table, a book open beside him to the right, the ruby glow of a glass within easy reach of his left hand. He removed his reading glasses as a gesture of transition between the solitary nature of study and the convivial discourse that attended dinner. He appeared unusually formal, something I attributed to Father's absence and the repressive shadow that fell on the house whenever his marginally uncoordinated step crossed the threshold.

'I trust you have spent the hours in profitable study,' he began. 'Reading is that process by which we receive another's thought in isolation, and discourse is that by which we reconvert that experience into something which becomes our own by virtue of considered reflection. I should like you to conceive of your studies in that light. You are at an age when sitting down seems a restraint on liberty, knowledge something to be acquired in old age, and when wisdom appears the dubious acme of those who have pursued an unadventurous life. These thoughts are, in their context, perfectly natural, but let me explain life to you in more accessible terms.'

Already I was focused elsewhere. What I knew was the intuitive, the unpredictable image clusters that constellated the unconscious. I could sense the rehearsed entry to his speech.

'In the ode of Pierre Ronsard's which we studied, you will remember how he discredited poetry as a prescription to poverty. Not even Anacreon, Simonides, Philetus or bacchylides, he says, can hope for anything but the erosion of their works by time. It is quite another order by which man advances to a position of office and security. It is with your father's wishes at heart that I advise you to pursue a course of study at Tarbes which provides for a profession. The imagination, or how shall I express it, a concern with the arts, leads invariably to the situation that Ronsard has described for us.'

What perturbed me more than the contents of his uninterrupted monologue was the allusion made to my secret writings. The suspicion I entertained of Monsieur Flammarion going through Father's papers extended to my own fear that he had access to my carefully concealed notebooks.

'Rhythm is in time what symmetry is in space,' I answered, hoping my vindication of poetry would go unobserved.

'At the Tarbes lycée', continued Monsieur Flammarion, 'you will be subjected to the disciplinarian values that demand a rigorous application to study. Your day will begin at 5.30 and finish at 7 p.m. The school allows no latitude for digression of any nature. But there is an achievement in that, a sense of living with and not outside of time.'

Already I felt trapped. The Atlantic beaches which were my sounding-board to the sky's blue deeps, the forest trees in which I perched like an animal in the heat, high over pools, the dreams I nurtured of disappearing into the interior of the country, of travelling as an entomologist in a canoe down the coils of the Amazon; the whole flight-paths of my childhood were being erased by the ordered precision of Monsieur Flammarion's dictates.

'Tarbes will prepare you for the Empire's new prosperity,' Monsieur Flammarion reflected over his wineglass. 'Change is instrumental in creating the momentum for still further change. When I stood in the esplanade des Invalides, under the sun of Austerlitz as we called it, and heard the salute of guns proclaim Louis-Napoleon's triumphant procession to the Place de l'Hôtel de Ville, almost eight years ago, it was for me still another beginning. And growing up is only an extension of this – you prepare yourself for what never happens, because, by the time it does, you have already outgrown it. The future will quickly displace your longing for the past.

'And there are things I should like to discuss with you, Ducasse, which don't fall into the natural order of our discourse,' Monsieur Flammarion ventured, his hand drawn to the fluted crystal of his wineglass.

In my imaginary world I was voyaging down the Amazon, penetrating a world of dense Bacaba palms, impenetrable forests, alligators snouting the scum.

'Your knowledge of history is still small,' he continued. 'A sense of the past, by which I mean the manner in which individuals seek to impose their own will on the prevailing ethos, is something one acquires in proportion to one's years. Whilst blood remains the discourse of history, we have still to attend to the cultural enlightenment of the mind.'

As I listened, I was reading the silent speech which is the true message of words. I had learnt how language is an accompaniment to thought and not the medium of its translation. The words themselves most often mislead and point to an inner dialogue – the message being in the undertow, like a hidden current chased out in the flow, so that speech involves the marriage of silences, the sympathetic attunement to dimensions of inner space. When you really picked up on a person's depths, you shared with him a redundance of words.

Behind Monsieur Flammarion's connected thoughts were the savage associations he did not dare articulate. I had read somewhere of how the convicted were sent to the guillotine barefooted, in a long white shirt, and concealed by a black, hooded veil which was lifted before the head was sliced into the blood-stained basket.

I could hear ships firing their cannons at sea. The screeching violin note of a rocket detonated high above the port in a shower of emerald stars. Monsieur Flammarion's perspective was narrowing. He was able to keep his eyes open only by concentrating on one thought at a time, sustaining its pitch, for fear that if he let it go he too would follow its extinction.

I was edging my way towards the irreversible flooding of his senses that would set me free to challenge the town's nocturnal alleys. When he left the room, a book wedged under one arm, I was conscious only of his attempt to sustain lucidity and of how for a moment he seemed to have preconceived my intentions, and to have lurched through my defences with the unreasoning drunkenness of a sailor come out of the harbour fog in order to menace.

I went upstairs, my body loaded with the dynamic impulse to take up with the drumbeat of the crowd. I knew that tonight delirium would reign in every quarter – a spontaneously choreographed hysteria. Roles would be reversed for the magic of the festivities; the poor would assume the mask of the rich, the slave that of a king, gender would be exchanged, and the crowds would follow the legend of 'O rei de Franca na ilha da Assombracao' – The King of France on the Haunted Island. The red, silver and white costumes would afford a brilliancy to the image of a boy-king, and to the legends of old black slave women from Maranhão, whose witchcraft changed a beautiful outcast slave into a silver snake.

From the balcony I could see that the light in Monsieur Flammarion's room was already extinguished. I inhaled the night scents of honeysuckle, fat lobes of perfume invaded by moths. How often I had stared from this window at a garden in which jewelled humming-birds sipped at the proliferation of scarlet roses.

Tonight would be the first stage of my leaving this house for ever. I knew in advance that my actions would not go unnoticed, despite the elaborate disguise I had prepared for the occasion. I unlocked a trunk and lifted out the papier-mâché pierrot's mask, cradling it like a death's head in my hands. The mask, with its black, down-turned lips, its gold tear sparkling on the right cheek, while a black butterfly occupied the left, represented the androgynous marriage of opposites.

I had prepared myself for the solemnity of this ritual. It was with perfect calm that I stepped out of my clothes and fastened the pearl buttons of my blouse. There was a fascination in studying my own face before replacing it with a mask. I had taken for granted features I rarely questioned. It was only now I realised my unnatural height and the pronounced stoop which, owing to my solitary life, had not yet grown to be a source of schoolboy ridicule. I did not recognise the person I was seeing, the hazel-green eyes that I used as the interpretative medium of conveying my emotions were objectively bewildered by my questioning. I had reversed the process of coming at the world, and confused my sensory responses by challenging them with a double.

My lank, blondish hair was unruly, and already I had developed the characteristic of pushing it back from my eyes with my left hand, a gesture that invariably infuriated my father. I was thin and my elongated fingers were fashioned for rings. It was a surprise to confront myself thus in reality, and disquieting to realise how great is the divide between the mental image we have of ourselves and the physical reality.

When I tried on the mask to accustom myself to this new identity, the experience was one of unity. I felt reconciled to a pre-existence. There was a sinking in, a realisation that the mask corresponded to the real me, and on its removal a corresponding sense of loss when confronted by my ordinariness.

The house was silent. I placed a grey topcoat over my sequined jacket and red tights, and prepared to carry the mask until I reached the outskirts of the town. What I should enter would be the collective spirit of the carnival, its primitive, animistic street ceremonials, the dark gods generating a sexual fever. Blood would be drawn in alleys, women posted up against walls and raped, chickens set fire to by thrown torches, horses would panic and jettison their riders, but the mob would be irrepressible, the spirit lifting them to a state of ecstasy that took in life and death as an inseparable experience.

Once clear of the house I broke into an exhilarated run. I crashed through opposing shrubland, tamarisk whiplashing my face. There was a molten red glow in the sky. Drifts of smoke swabbed my lungs so that I choked on the acrid reek of bonfires. In my confusion I half stumbled over a couple making love beside the road, shapely dark legs knotted round a white waist, the fingers travelling up and down the spine as though playing a guitar. The countryside was constellated with couples abandoned to a spontaneous orgiastic coupling. Overhead the sky was lit by whizzing racemes of red lobelias.

The journey I had to make on foot was longer than I had anticipated, and I kept up a half-run, the past beginning to stream through my mind with a concentrated and indelible imagery. I was again experiencing the terrible silence in the house on the day that Mother had gone missing. It was that which told me she was dead. I could see myself going out into a garden I no longer recognised. On that day I had run towards the beach without seeing. They were still there in my unconscious, the group of native fishermen squatting down on the sand, contracted into a tightly bunched ring. Alma was visible amongst them, her orange sheath pronounced against the azure. My way there had been through a jerky visual field: Mother's blotched face and matted hair, her waterlogged clothes clinging to her like wrack beached by a wave, blood streaming from an ankle. These impossible transformations were being re-enacted again. The words Célestine-Jacquette had bitten into my mind and were repeated by scalding tears. They had placed her face down on the sand and one of the fishermen was pumping her back, forcing the water from her mouth as if she were a fish. I wanted to scream now as I had then. Alma had pulled me away, ripping my hand, tenting me in the warmth of the same body that had come to me this afternoon dressed in my mother's clothes to consummate the incestuous union which had never been realised. And the drag back across the beach, my feet moving of their own accord in response to Alma's rhythm, the attenuated umbilical that still existed as a lifeline between Mother and me, thinning towards the inevitable break. I had tried to run back in the opposite direction to which I was running now. It was the force of Alma's outspread palm, creating a solar roar in my ear, which had stopped me. The force of her blow had spun my head round, so that I had followed in blind obedience, her heart and muscles pumping for us both, the incline up the littoral staggering her forceful drive, but her grip on me had the strangulating effect of a liana, a tentacular handhold pulling me up out of a dark crater into the bright green sunshine of the early afternoon.

My breath was laboured. And now as I reached the outskirts of the town I was visibly disturbed. The dramatic events of the day, the anticipated dangers of the carnival night, the breathlessness of my flight, all of these factors had contributed to my hallucinated vision. The flashbacks so disorientated me that it seemed I had never left the beach and was impaled on a white blade of light mirrored off that violent noonday sea.

I posted myself up against a wall and urinated. A red papier-mâché dragon was being canted from a flat roof-top while balloons in the shape of silver sea-horses lifted fluctuatingly into the black night-sky. The values of a society were being stood upside-down – the money won by such hardship, such minted sweat in the face of crops, was being blown sky-high in the ecstatic evaluation of the present. There was only 'now', the sudden immersion in pure being. Every societal privilege would be dissolved in the light of a reversion to primordial chaos.

I began running again, swooping into an alley, adopting my mask for the first time and conscious of the freedom it permitted. I was now breathing and living through the medium of a mask: I had become somebody else. Death was everywhere in the form of paper and sugar-candy skulls, skeletons with fireworks shooting through their hollow eye-sockets.

The town was written in my nerves, and I was conscious without having visited many of its quarters of the potential it offered for the sublimation of unconscious desires. I could hear the mamba beat accompanying the central exhibit of headless horses reverberating from the town centre. The negro primitivism displayed in the rhythm of the music was expressive of pain, revolt and abandonment. It was beginning to work itself into my blood and transform my body into the willowy fluid organism of someone motivated by their deepest primal instincts.

People were grouped on balconies, playing guitars, exchanging an endless relay of jokes, so that the discordance was on two levels, the delirium of the street rising to meet the hysterical crescendo of roof-top carnival. Everything and everyone seemed to be straining towards the sky, where poinsettias suddenly flared open in the blue-black.

Tonight those who believed in the gold-mines at Ophir, and

how Solomon sent treasure-ships up the Amazon to the Japurá river, would re-enact the subliminal location of treasure. The charged air wired me to my own individualised vision of the universe. I was a shaman capable of turning into a werewolf and drinking the blood of my aggressor earlier in the day, and able to complete the ecstatic journey to the sky or the descent into the underworld to reclaim my mother's soul.

In a synchronised outburst of firework salvoes I could see the red beam of the lighthouse perched on the ruins of an old fortress five hundred feet above the harbour, directing its radial light across the night seas. For a moment I entertained the idea of climbing to those heights and celebrating the carnival from that elevation, but the momentum of the crowds dragged me back into the tributaries that seemed magnetised to a common centre – the oneiric vision of the child-king drawn by red-blanketed horses.

I moved forward and found myself wedged in the spinal undulations of a chequered serpent, a garnet-eyed, fang-flickering head that raised its phallic crest to the stars. We were of one movement, a unified trance in which the intermeshing of minds found its counterpart in the mamba's rhythmic beat. The fear of death that had so heightened my senses earlier in the day had temporarily vanished. I found myself manoeuvring between a bull's head and the silver plumes of a bird-mask, my pulsebeat seeming to resonate from the drumskin.

The great train of the living were filing towards the dead. Tonight there would be an exchange of identities, a crossing of frontiers; some would disappear like the wild swan and others would come back, and the transference of identities would be known to neither. When I forced myself free of the mesmerised train, my body was still answering to the music. I had shed my heritage; lit coals twinkled beneath my dancing feet – I was a humming-bird darting through the yawning jaws of a jaguar.

I got into an alley where two masked figures beat out a rhythm on tambourines and danced round a black mulatto. Behind that a violet, turbaned head was engaged in fellatio; the glittering, beehived mask working with the motion of a potter's hand-shaping craft on an abandoned partner in a doorway.

I began deliberately to seek out the person who had confronted me in the alley behind the market-place. A desperate need to fulfil something unrealised in me compelled me to rush sharply from alley to alley. Blinded by smoke I found myself abruptly projected towards the main exhibit – the frisky, nightmarish advance of headless horses, red plumes combed back from their manes, a snake and a bull flanking them on either side. In my confusion I imagined being dragged under the float, trampled by the stampeding crowds. I flickered momentarily towards the vortex before the adrenalin-flash hit my nerves, having me catapult high to the right of the advancing float, my body awkwardly thrashing above the shoulders of the oncoming dancers, flailing, heaped, and finally nosediving into the maelstrom, firm hands righting my way up without faltering in the procession's march, so that I was jammed into a place that wasn't a space at all, my ribs bruised, my lungs forcing for air, my arms locked against my sides. I was being dragged forward like a dead branch on the spine of a fast-flowing stream. The music and accompanying delirium of bodies exploded in my head. My direction had been turned around, so that I went with the current and not against it. I should have to work my way five to the left to be free of the constrictive ruck, to punch a gap through the log-jam to the crowds lining the pavement and beat a solitary retreat to the old quarter.

Furnacing in the crush I imagined the white, hissing cloud rising off water boiling in a volcano crater. My height allowed me to periscope, and through our position close to the front I could see that the whole procession was going to have to turn left to advance down the high street towards the American and Grand Hotels, and in the slowing of pace necessary to achieve this I planned to force myself out of the asphyxiating crush. At the exact moment of pause, when the drum fractionally decreased in its beat and our line came to an illusory standstill, I worked my way through the slight gap that opened in the wedge, my elbows jutting in my ricochet from one body to another, my fierce, relentless urgency to bullet clear leaving me winded, my head spinning, before I was free to balance upright, hands stretched out to a wall as the full sweep of the processional rounded the corner.

I moved away from the crowd into a side-street. From a balcony overhead I could hear the unrestrained orgasmic throatiness of a woman ascending the pleasure-scale to climax.

I examined the tear in my mask, flinching at the same time from fear of exposing my identity, and traced out a lesion that could have been inflicted by a knife. The features I had admired for so long, and come to assimilate as my true identity, had been symbolically wounded. It was the laceration intended by my armed opponent at noon.

I refitted the mask to my face, my eyes depending for sight on a restricted central vision. At every corner I expected to encounter my fixation: the cerise mask lowered, the scarlet jacket pinched to outline the figure, the legs poured into yellow tights. The shock I had experienced earlier in the day over the confused sex of my opponent had come to be mediated by the realisation that someone could be both male and female. The core of my juvenile sexuality was expanding from a molten amorphousness to settle in the mould of an ambivalent object of desire. Alma's love-making had left me unsatisfied; her flesh had suffocated me without pronouncing any clear definition to which I wished to hold. She had swum above my transfixed body in the position I had imagined a man would adopt.

I clawed my way through dense smoke to a gap in the darkness. The overhanging houses were familiar, and I was convinced that I had come full circle to end up again in the alley behind the Plaza de Independencia. Above me music issued from the roof-tops. Guitars responded to the mood dictated by the singer, black with the slow melancholy of rains falling in a mountain pool, or wild with the wing-clapping beat of flamingos rising above a lake.

I came to a dead halt in the middle of the road and stood there listening to my thoughts beat out the tune of their dialogue. I dropped to one knee to examine a tear in my scarlet tights, my right hand exploring my raised left kneecap, while the left went wide of the leg in support, fingers splayed and suddenly hot with a nick of scalding blood as a stiletto whistled to a quivering vertical in the dusty V between my little and fourth finger. I jolted back, mouth open, eyes staring, my nerves electrified, frazzled by the invasive leap from security to danger. I had been found out in my own thoughts, knife-punched back to a reality in which I was without defences. My focus was narrowed to the thin, tapering blade, as though the fitted handle constituted the polarity for my being, a fixed identity that I had gone down to find, and once having discovered could live by no other recognition. I was waiting for the challenge that never came. In my stylised, rigid pose, I seemed to be prolonging a choreographed movement, the completion of which depended on an invisible partner.

I turned fractionally on my pivotal heel in the direction from which the knife had been placed. Agonisingly, I moved round the fractions of an imaginary circle enclosing me. I felt like someone who, crouched on a circular disc of ice and rotating slowly, comes to realise that he faces a blue ocean on all sides. I could see a shadow projecting from a doorway. It was still, superimposed on the road, the angular boniness of the human thinned out to an ink-wash. It was the laugh that greeted me first, an uncontained falsetto that synchronised with the duration of a comet's whizzing tail. Then I saw him, the mask trained on me as it had been earlier in the day, the red jacket rain-dropped with brilliants, the livid colours sported on the enigma within. He was standing with his back to a wooden door, invincibly cool, calculated to threaten by the very quiet of his composure. Something within me was magnetised by this hybrid creature. I felt my nerves pick up on that attraction; I was being drawn towards him the way an animal hypnotised by fear goes complacently towards the jaws that have tracked it across country. As I began to move, so he disappeared upstairs, his illusory figure gone with provocative menace.

I got up, over-exposed by the magnified inner lens through which I watched my awkward movements, knowing there could be no going back on this, and that if I did not follow, I should be hunted through the night as the sacrificial victim of the carnival.

The Eye 4

Isidore Ducasse must have left the house some time between 11 p.m. and midnight. In this my instincts served me right. I anticipated that his reasons for getting caught up in the carnival's delirium had to do with the figure X rather than the spirit of entertainment.

Mixing in the harbour area earlier that night I was fortunate enough to encounter an American acquaintance of your son's. Slightly intoxicated, given to garrulity, the man was drinking vermouth in a quayside bar. Dressed in a white panama, the man made no attempt to conceal the bundles of green dollars that loaded his pockets.

After striking up a degree of easy trust I got on to the subject of your son. It turns out that Isidore Ducasse goes under the name of Comte de Lautréamont in these casual encounters. He adopts this pseudonym presumably to avoid the risk of being traced. You will agree that it is a refined art of duplicity for one so young. The man was guarded about his relations with your son. My pretending to be in sympathy with his nature, and recommending places where he could form further attachments, met with suspicion. There is always a reserve to a drunk, an area of experience which he feels is being threatened by his dissociation.

What I did manage to ascertain is that money changes hands in the relationship between Isidore Ducasse and the various foreigners whom he meets in Montevideo. These sums are either the exaction of blackmail, money paid for favours in the town – remember, your son is in a privileged position given your office – or payment in respect of contraband.

On carnival night Isidore Ducasse arrived at the Bista del Mar in a state of exhaustion and evident dissipation. His harlequin's costume was torn at one knee, his pierrot's mask was cracked. I have still to ascertain where in Montevideo he procured this costume, but a systematic check should supply me with the dealer. Your son's height, his stoop, the unkempt manner in which he keeps his long hair, his self-absorption and nervous hesitancy of speech mark him out amongst the residents. So too an intellectual modesty which points to an expansive capacity he conceals. He shows signs too of having picked up as a speech affectation the old Bonapartist terms adopted by Gustave Flammarion.

He stayed at X's for over an hour and a half, finally leaving the house at great speed and continuing beyond my reach until I ascertained that he had returned home. I leave his purpose at the Bista del Mar to your assessment.

A source of continuous frustration is my inability to be able to resolve your son's duplicity by isolating specific acts. His personal life still remains one of conjecture. I hope, however, to be able to report in time on more explicit actions of a sexual or criminal nature.

Chapter 4

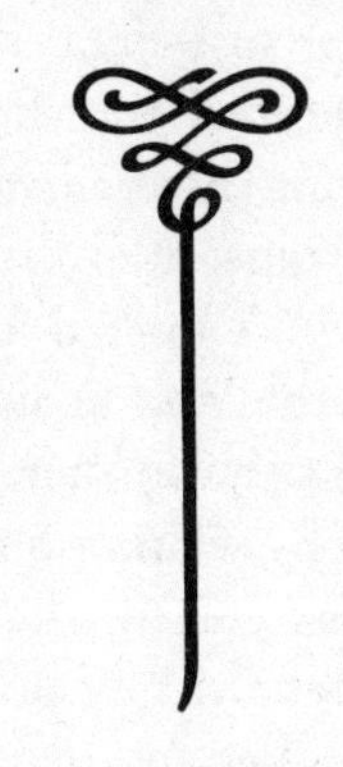

The way up was lit by the orange glow of a lamp placed at the top of the first floor. I was the wolf who had lived in the sheep's belly as I realised the metamorphosis I was still in the act of completing. I had crossed the frontiers of identity; my oval face was not the product of my parents but the habitable construct of the imagination.

The balls of my feet were silk as I took the stairs, familiarising myself with each flaw in the stone, stair-sills polished by tired feet, quick feet, the drag-back of lethargy, elation of a lyric skip. I was coming at the light without heredity or past. If I had boundaries, they had been stretched to universal proportions: my foot rested on the blue spin of the globe and not the bevelled join of a spiral stair. As I came up level with the first floor I could see a door left ajar, a pink sash of light spilling from beneath the jamb. As I hung back on the outside, I was aware of nothing that had brought me here, dislodged me from my parental home; a boy on the threshold of being sent away for a privileged education in Europe was facing the entrance to a room lit with the smokiness of a hole in the Dantean pit.

When I pushed the door to I could not see him at first. The whitewashed room was heaped with flowers which must have been dragged up here from the carnival streets. Narcissi, blue irises, red and pink carnations, lilies shaped like cornucopias. It had not occurred to me as I looked around the room at the roughly made wooden table and chairs, at the coarse cotton curtains drawn back from a four-poster bed which occupied half the room, that he might be waiting outside, higher up on the stairs, hardly breathing as I entered the trap.

The room appeared devoid of all possessions. The blistered spines of a few books bleached by the sunlight, an insignificant rosewood crucifix, a bottle and glass on the table grouped with the self-conscious isolation of a composition arranged for a still life, were at first all that registered in the muted light. I stood there afraid I would lose my energy charge, and acutely aware that I was for the first time in my life an intruder. I was on the inside of the night, from where the street proceedings took on a new dimension. I was at just sufficient a remove to allow for detachment. I felt as though I had withdrawn into an ante-room on the occasion of some great historic decision, and that for a brief interlude the surf roar of the mob had subsided, while the child hot from the warming-pan was swaddled in a cloak of fleurs-de-lis before being lifted to the attendant crowd.

Time was measured by the racing heartbeats that drummed in my ears. I felt humbled by the simplicity of the room, its expedient frugality, the bare wooden floors where the tumbled flower sprays had not been spread. My mind was beginning to assimilate the room, absorb it the way water diffuses a blue spiral of paint from a brush-tip. I was filling up with it, clouding at the base, when I heard the door click shut behind me.

'And so you came,' a voice said, without waiting for me to turn round, so that I continued to face the blue window-frame with its shooting parabolas of streaming lights. 'I knew you would come back. You see, I have been watching you for a long time. There is something that draws attention to itself in a young man who doesn't fit into an established role in life. I have seen the places you visit when you come to town – the abattoir, the alleys, and how you wander in and out of the big hotels. You are looking for something I found a long time ago.'

The voice that addressed me was slow, articulate, drawn up out of the chest so that the words seemed to have been spoken deep down before rising to the surface. It was as though this was the depth of their consideration. They were aired to a secret confidant, an invisible intermediary, before being directed towards their eventual recipient.

I did not have to turn round; the harlequined figure went wide of me, coming at me slowly from the far side of the circular table. The cerise mask was still in place, the voice slightly distorted by the mouth's restricted opening. I had the feeling that the impersonation was the real being, and that like myself the occupant of the mask had come to realise in his cosmetic persona the true nature of his identity. In this we were twins and in all other respects strangers.

'Why have you been watching me?' I found myself asking, the words grouping of their own accord, insignificant, no longer even pertinent to the occasion as he sat squat on the four-poster bed watching me, composed as if he knew I had to stay in order to find out the reason for his motivation.

'The first time I saw you, you were on the beach,' the voice took up. 'You were naked because of the warmth and privacy. I was higher up than you and looking down at the bay. I know this coast, contour by contour, its deeps and shallows, and the place where a boat can put in before crossing the estuary to Rio. You have to know these things if you live as I do. The people one encounters on this coast are soldiers with girls from the town, tourists, men who are out there because they cannot always formulate their need into words, dissidents waiting for a cause, an occasional coastguard. You were out there but you were really inside yourself. I could see that it would not have mattered if the shoreline had disappeared.

'In my life you have a purpose for being somewhere – time represents money. But you were like a child mesmerised by fire. I wanted to break into your mind and discover the secret. And I was disturbed by your committing your thoughts to paper. Once they are expressed, words give you an identity. I have never wanted to be traced. I have not left any words, not even a signature. If you live by ear, people do not remember what you say, but you learn from their expression.

'When you left the beach, I followed you. I traced you back to the white house in which I imagined you lived with your parents. I used to look up at the windows at night and imagine you alone in your room, probably sitting at a table, reading or writing. I got to know which one of the two was your father. The other one was already known to me by sight.'

As I listened to the voice inform me of my life, both in its inner and outer contents, I realised that my childhood isolation was illusory, and that someone else had accompanied me on its journey. All of those days I had luxuriated in the azure cove, I had been watched. A contained penumbra had set up its own tent on the sand. I could imagine the quiet he must have instated, toning even the volume of his thoughts to a minimal pitch. He had lived through the aperture of his eye, the targe regulating the light, his visual field intuiting my need to be alone.

'When you began to be attracted to the local abattoir, I followed you with renewed interest. I could see you were repelled by what you witnessed, but still you had to put yourself through the experience. I tracked you there. I watched the sweat-patches darken under your shirt when you removed your jacket, and the blood drain from your face when the bellowing hulk resisted the thrown noose. You must have thought those journeys the most secret of your life. But we are never free. Someone is always watching, and in the end we put on masks so as to be so conspicuous that people no longer look at us.'

His voice needled my memory cells, imploding a series of depth flashes, silver bubbles that raced to the surface, each encapsulating a particular visual image.

'You are lying,' I shouted, my anger feeding on his incisive tone. 'You don't know the first thing about me.'

'I also know about your mother,' the voice continued with quiet assertion. He had tucked his legs under him and was shaking out the sparkles on his coat.

'I was there that day they fished her out of the sea. You forget my time is spent on the coast. You are not the only reason for my being there. They call me the Queen of Hearts. You cannot see, but my back is tattooed with red hearts. Time for me is mediated by action. For you it is a process of holding a mirror to your thoughts. Out there they would call you Narcissus.'

'But what is out there?' I questioned. 'Who are you that you follow me?'

'I'm the Queen of Hearts, as I told you. And you are Isidore Ducasse, son of a French diplomat. You will never lose your stoop. They will mock you for it at school, and when you run away they will pelt your spine with rotten fruit. And then you will plot against them in secret. I know your sort. You dream of savage reprisals, worlds built out of words. And that's what people fear most, because once they are written down, they cannot be destroyed.'

I was unnerved by his easy shift between eloquence and a life-style that was unknown to me. He seemed to be able to stitch the two together and with a tailor's chalk and pins create an invisible seam. I imagined his body like that; the male and female elements brought together in a defiant challenge.

'I have experienced life in a way that you can never know,' he was saying. 'I was at one time part of a travelling circus, then I followed in the wake of the Argentinian Army all the way up the Cuyaba river to Paraguay. What I wanted from life was the knowledge that I was participating in time. And the greater the involvement, the more I realised that men paid to escape from reality. I already knew of the drug peyote, and of its power to induce hallucination, and of opium that the French sailors trafficked along the coast. There are ways of earning money which have people come back for more. You learn that out on the coast.'

I wanted to run, but my legs had solidified. I found myself backing off into a chair, trying to imagine the pictures inside his head as he was reliving them.

'I have travelled all over the continent,' he resumed. 'Right to the interior and the lower reaches of the Amazon. There the wall of trees cuts off the sky. And the nights. The black stuff is so thick one crouches to a fire. There are always Indians or natives watching – tricking through the undergrowth like snakes. No one thinks to come out alive.'

I could sense that behind his eyes everything was standing out in its retrieval, huge, creased from long storing, fluid, wet with the primal colours of the unconscious.

'You have not realised', he was saying, 'how much attention I have paid you. What I have known of life I have come to channel into an eye that concentrates on finding out how much of myself there is in another. Once I am aware of that, I know how much space I have to fill. The Queen of Hearts is about finding levels. Because you live so much in the centre of yourself, I found it hard to get in.'

I kept wondering how much longer I should stay. This man had tracked me, and I had the image of a deer feeling the weight of an eye on it, trying to brush it off like a fly, but the eye sticking, burning in round its target.

'When your mother drowned,' he said, 'I knew something had broken in you. Your face as you came up off the beach was so near to me that I thought you had seen me. And then I realised you could not see anything. You were distracted. I knew it was your father you were blaming. They had fought, the two of them. I had watched their altercations build to blows. The Queen of Hearts is always filling in spaces. Already you know something about your parents that you did not before. I could tell you the hidden side to everyone. There is a monster that sleeps in all of us, one eye closed and one awake. I am the personification of the evil you would like to eliminate in yourself. If I killed you with this knife, it would not be murder but suicide. Only the law does not see things like that. It insists on punishing one being for the ritual self-murder of the other.'

The pressure was building in me. It was all coming back: Mother's interminably long visits to friends, my father's hostile silences when she was away, that cold reservation I had come to equate with an over-diligent concern with his career. His manner was to dismiss me from his left-hand side by turning his head wide and short of my eyes. The past struck my chin like a wave.

'Now that I have brought you face to face with yourself,' he resumed, 'you are silent. You could reverse the situation, only my confrontation with myself occurred a long time ago. I was working in the Pampas. One day I had to lasso a small black stallion, one I had marked out as recalcitrant. I got it while it was grazing, and although it resisted, I managed to saddle it. I cut the creature so hard and repeatedly with a whip that I bloodied its right flank. Whether it was the heat or the exertion I do not know, but suddenly my arm was not completing the action, and when the horse swung round, fixing whatever it saw as me, it was myself I recognised in that stare. The furious animosity we shared for each other had resulted in this exchange of identities.'

His hand was unsteady as he aligned the neck of a bottle of tequila with a glass. When the liquor hit his nerves, he caught his breath. We sat in the blue corolla of an expansive pink flower as a firework detonated from a roof-top. The excitement that had brought me here in defiance of danger was diminishing. I was coming down after the blinding flash that had uprooted me.

'There will be victims tonight,' he continued. 'Knife-clashes, hands burnt by explosives, those whose bodies cannot live up to the dictates of the drug, and I have marked them all. I was in the streets yesterday and today and my look singled out those who will die. What happened to me today was the result of a police reinforcement. The policeman who dared look at me will go on doing so until he is mad, like an animal staring at a fire.'

There was a pause in his monologue. He cradled his head in his hands, supporting the fatigue that showed in his restrained body movements. The line of his body was accentuated by the tight fit of his clothes. He had a schoolboy's slight waist, but his shoulders and diaphragm were powerfully developed in contrast to his stick-thin legs, his gracefully elongated fingers. With each shot of tequila he seemed to spiral up a scale of blue-spirited flame. I could see him thinking behind that fire-screen. I had the feeling he wanted to blow a hole through the back of his mind with pure sensation. I could see the outline of his sex through his dancer's tights. Tubular, extended, aroused, it was the shape of a cactus, only it dragged globular roots in its distension. The angle of his body made it clear to me that he was inviting, provoking a sexual advance. I remained fixed, contemplating my flight – a hunched, helter-skelter dash through the alleys in the hope of finding concealment in the procession.

I was steeling myself to make a break and run out into the whirling flux. I felt as though I had been hooked through the lip, and that only by tearing loose and running with my wound could I convince myself of the reality of what had happened. The carnival was breaking down individual barriers; the great collective, animistic spirit moved forward like a flood-tide racing for its high-water mark. Whatever lived in the process of still becoming, the whole explosive primal world of the extinct, and the monstrous try-outs still to be conceived, rioted through the paper walls of my skull. Life was flowing into death, its opposite and complement, and carrying off those it demanded as a blood sacrifice, and those who lacked the psychic defence to withstand the pressure of that tide.

I knew that this man wanted my blood as a propitiation to the dark gods. Alma had told me stories of magic transformation, whereby the sorcerer adopts the form of an animal, a werewolf or a dog to drink the blood of his enemies. In ecstatic trance he then journeys out of himself, carried across the sky on an eight-legged horse. Under threat, I tried to imagine my own death, the journey back to the creative consciousness, the dream source, the immersion in being that was no longer particularised by action. It seemed impossible that one could arrive there from the severance of an artery by a knife-blade. Rather I visualised the encounters of the hero, the ordeals to be undertaken and surmounted before death became a reality.

I could feel my blood recharging, the current humming in my nerves. His jacket front was stained with liquor escaped from an awkward mouthpiece.

'You won't forget the Queen of Hearts,' he shrieked, his shrillness collapsing back into a bottle-tilted choke. 'I could make you somebody in this world, in this God-forsaken, thieving world. . . .'

His hand went down to his sex, and he simultaneously pushed his legs out in front of him and arched his back against the heaped pillows. I could sense his withdrawal into fantasy, the insertion of a film between himself and the blur I must have come to represent. I imagined myself as a black, white and red night-moth, oval face tilted partially askew, suspended in his focus as a recessive image, fore and hind wings raised, antennae bristling from the down-turned corners of my black mouth. It was odd to think that while I sat stable, I must have appeared fragmented, oscillating from left to right like water shaken in a glass.

When I stood up he made no effort to counteract my intentions. I had floated wide of his orbit, and his hand worked with a regulated monotony at his sex. He was like a man who had forgotten the reason for his words, having stalled in mid-sentence. I was suddenly disposable, anonymous, incidental to his self-gratifying lust. I took one step back and then another, testing out what I supposed was a trap, expecting at any moment to be paralysed into obedience by his dictates.

A third and a fourth step; I had the impression I was learning to walk for the first time, my nerves waking to a post-hypnotic animation. I could feel the balls of my feet touch the wooden boards with the sensitivity of a pianist's fingers.

A fifth step and a sixth. The door was behind me. I had only to blow out its frame to realise the influx of smoke-saturated air. In my mind I was already face-up against the whitewashed, rectilinear walls of our house, my fingers finding the unlocked sash of the library window, the house dormant, not a light or sound other than the reverberation of surf in the cove.

My face was cold-dropped with sweat beneath my mask. The knife was marginally out of reach to his right, the blade rhyming with the room's atmospherics, a small, lethal, useless thing he would not have time to punch between my ribs. A seventh and eighth step. I was turning the world upside-down in my head.

His breath was beginning to saw; I could hear it intensifying with the crisis in his body. A mosquito trapped in the room irascibly planed the ceiling, nose-diving into the lamp, then, setting off on a circuitous reconnaissance, blundered from obstacle to obstacle in an electric whine.

In the process of thinking about flight I had become the reality of my thought. In the power of my removal from the room, I was conscious only of the irrevocable decision I had made to risk acting. The stairs no longer appeared those I had quizzed with such caution on my arrival; rather they were impediments to my hurry, a spiral cut into a well-shaft that seemed rooted in a ravine. I slewed from wall to wall in the scrambled urgency, bruising my ribs, taking the last four steps in a lifting jump as I choppered out through the door, colliding, weaving, ducking between wedges of people whose movements were earthed in the dance's sexual rhythm. My bony angularity, my headlong rush contradicted the pattern; I was too visible in my blinding terror.

I tilted at breakneck speed through a troop of chequered clowns, red bulbous noses, bangles of straw hair, mouths painted red to the chin, sash-sized blue satin bows attached to hooped collars. The town I knew so well seemed to have increased in size and complexity. A drunk lurched out of a doorway, his muzzy baritone cursing me, his imprecations following me the length of the road until I got into a side-street. At every turning I expected him to appear, his sequined mask bringing me to a stumbling halt. I could hear the sea; the groundswell of the Atlantic plotting the rhythm of its tides, that familiar music which had come to be associated with the movements of my blood. Its serene surf-line was breaking around the coast, rolling in the shallows like a playful white tiger. I knew that once I had picked up on its metronomic irregularities, its variance of longshore pitch, I was safe. Space with its flawless blue panes was a window on infinity. I had only to think of it to be there. Monsieur Flammarion's endless descriptions of enfilading Napoleonic troops, frogged blue jackets dusted by smoke on the veldt, the sky lit with the thunder-flash of cannons, came back to me as I imagined myself deserting the field under pressure of the redcoat cavalry cutting through a foot-sliding, bullet-holed artillery. Fireworks detonated above the harbour. At each renewed explosion I expected the black night-sky to cave in like a shop-front. I dared not turn round for fear of pursuit. I ran until I dropped into high, cool grasses. The air sparkled with fireflies, fizzing, electric twitches crackling from point to point. Frogs and toads had set up a discordantly gruff chorus in the grassland in answer to the monotonous chirr of cicadas. I could feel the earth laying claim to me, dragging me down, so that my hands were like the trailing roots of a water-lily.

I took off the sodden, torn mask which had claimed the full power of my frenzy, and crumpled it with my fist in the grass. The town and its nocturnal brilliance were behind me. There was already the promise of dawn in the east – a green, pulsating island of light dilating in the blue-black pool of space.

I knew I should have to leave Montevideo to be free of the Queen of Hearts and his obsession with the details of my life. I imagined him lying dead drunk on his counterpane, the bottle having rolled to the floor and leaked its contents. He would be breathing heavily through the restrictions of his mask. He would wake at noon, his head hammered by bruises inflicted by the light. His grease-paint would have run like candle-wax down the side of a holder.

When I got back, the house was silent. A cock was opening up at the watery skyline. I could hear the waves dragging their ball gowns into the cove. I lay face down on my bed, too tired to sleep. In my semiconscious state Father was a black sphinx, his lion's body curled up on the divan. The Queen of Hearts was watching him through a window, undeterred by the species of his change. When the latter pressed his face against the glass, Father licked his hands and assumed an air of feline diffidence. The surf was beginning to flood as I fell asleep.

The Eye 5

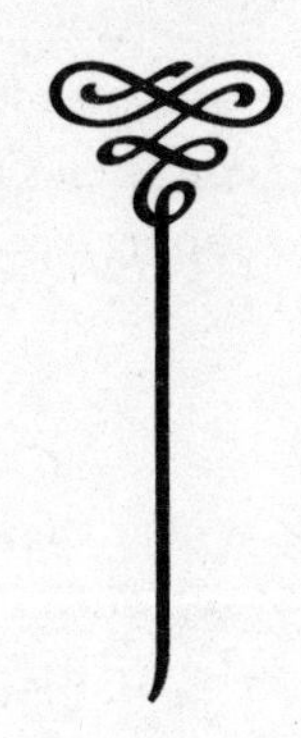

What makes my job so hard is your son's refusal to exteriorise motives. He appears lazy but is probably better informed than most adults. He adopts indifference to his future, which in turn may suggest a concealed strategy.

At times I feel that it is he who is following me rather than I him. The only inconsistency in his life is that of secrecy.

I have only small things to report. I contrived to get into conversation with a friend of your son's called Paul Lafon. On the pretext of engaging him in talk about a performance of Sophocles' *Oedipus Rex*, which is to be given by an amateur group with whom your son has connections, I was able by insinuating myself as a friend of the director's to inquire after Isidore Ducasse.

It appears that your son is disliked for his diffidence. Lafon speaks with reservation of your son's reluctance to share and penchant for incidents of minor cruelty. He treats his few acquaintances with an unpleasant dismissiveness, telling one that he will drown, and in the process undergo the torment of seeing himself repeat every wrong act, including masturbation, and another that he will ride out of grassland into a deep, red marsh and drown in a state of paralysis on horseback.

Such inventions suggest a dangerous imagination at work, and one that it is imperative to suppress.

Chapter 5

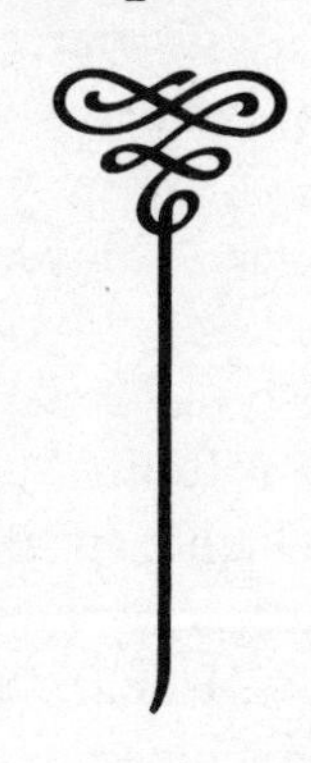

Monsieur Flammarion sat looking out of the study window at whitecaps snow the ultramarine bay. His attention, which should have been given to Father, found relief in a distraction designed to accentuate his seriousness and to impress on me the notion that the views expressed met with only his partial approval. His tight-sleeved, midnight-blue frock-coat reached to the knees of his putty-coloured trousers, overscored with an orange and brown check. His hands toyed with a red Moroccan binding. He seemed vague, watery, but vitally alert to Father's speech.

Father stood behind his walnut desk, shoulders raised to the pads of his grey serge coat, his black silk bow matched by the sash across his double-breasted waistcoat. He was ludicrously pompous, his rotund belly forced out in the manner of a bird puffing itself up by way of defence. I could see him rehearsing his sentences, considering his gambit, trying already to divorce himself from the significance of his words.

'Ducasse,' he began, 'we have after careful consideration decided on the expedient of sending you to Tarbes in the hope that education will act as a corrective to your ways. Reports have come to me from various sources of your idleness, your association with the town. Besides, you will have heard of the cholera outbreak in the city. By midsummer the dead will be dragged out to die in the street. I myself shall cross the estuary to Buenos Aires, and if necessary go on from there to Chile.

'You'll be sent to the lycée and there you must educate yourself to provide for your future.'

As I grew dissociated, so Father appeared to be talking in a low key. He was miming the slow, cud-chewing gape of a cow turned lazy by the afternoon heat. I imagined a swarm of irate bees filtering into his throat, punching the sensitive tissue with their scalding stings.

'I understand that, further to your discredit, you have been associating with people outside your class. Your liberties must be punished or they will increase....'

I drifted in and out of the monologue. Father appeared gouty, apopleptic, rancorous. His sandy moustache was flecked with steel and had coarsened into a beaver-muff, concealing the upper lip. He had become his own audience, and in the tone of his voice I caught what must have been the measure of his cruelty to Mother. I wanted to oppose him with the incidents told me by the Queen of Hearts. And in their having come to me second-hand they would be the more terrible, for their exaggerations would conform to the intentions he had wished to consummate but never succeeded in completing. I sensed the coward in him – the man who had beaten her with the flat of his open hands. His actions were written up in primary colours on the walls. Mother was sand-blasted by his towering fury, hypnotised into waiting for the concussive blow.

'You must prepare yourself to leave within the month,' Father was saying. Colour flooded his cheeks, decanted itself like port into his complexion. A purple vine of dilated veins showed in his forehead.

If I had tilted at him, head-butting, hollowing his inflated belly, he would have struggled on the carpet, calling down blood on the head of the son he had insulted. Monsieur Flammarion retained his pose with the concentration of an artist's model. He had drawn his hands together and sat half attentive, half distracted by the blue flashings of the bay in the window. The light jumped against the glass like the rainbowed agony of a boarded fish. His eyes watered; he was wincing under his characteristic role of wishing to remain neutral.

I watched the bowstring in Father's leg imperceptibly quiver, and the tension simultaneously trace out the ripple of a nerve in his left cheek. He pulled up short, as though blocking any evidence of the fractional disorder. He was like a man exposed by a fixed spotlight. His indignation demanded he face the wall. I listened for the explosion, but instead he jerked for air like someone struck in the pit of the stomach.

When he turned round, his face was a bloodless full moon. 'Get up to your room and stay there,' he ordered in the hushed, peremptory tone of a man alarmed by a shock that has taken place in his body. I was waiting for him to crash like a tree. Instead he seemed to be holding on to something inside which kept him from falling. A spar, a fireman's handhold across a ledge, a branch jutting out above a canyon. He must have been anticipating the recurrence, the blood-speck that would eclipse his consciousness.

I closed the door quietly and went up to my room. The measured pendulum of our mahogany Empire grandfather clock with its maritime panels drummed with the inexorable finality of time that outlives us all. I was already making notes on my observations, filling exercise books with my own thoughts and those of others who intersected with the plane of my poetic vision. I liked to imagine I was the club-footed Lord Byron at Newstead Abbey, rejected, departing from England in high dudgeon, planning my revenge on the world with whip-cutting savagery. Written in my nerves was the message of a universal cataclysm. I imagined a black corona surrounding a red sun, white cities landsliding into the sea, and men making for the deserts of the world under a rain of meteors. There would be lions in the street, eyes watching from pebbles and writing in the dust. The Name would be written by the wind on a dune in the Sahara.

I lay on my bed and scanned the precocity of a passage I had entered into my notebook on the preceding night.

> He buries his head up to his neck in the tunnels of a hole; but conscience volatilises this head-down ostrich-trick. The hole disappears and its ether-drop expands to a series of light-rays deployed like a flight of curlews swooping down on lavender; and man, wide-eyed, comes face to face again with his double. I have seen him heading for the sea, scaling a rocky promontory, lashed by a white eyebrow of surf, and project himself like an arrow into the waves. But the miracle is this: the corpse reappeared the next day on the surface, dragged in with the high tide's jettisoned flotsam. The man detached himself from his body's imprint on sand, wrung the water out of his hair, and silently returned to his way of life.

My imaginative faculty was inexhaustible. My concern was not with inherited worlds and the monotonous duplication of reality, but with worlds created by the imagination. And beyond? Europe was a minotaur I had to appease. The rank, horned bull's head would attempt to gore me before I could appeal to the similarity of our bodies. Cenotaphs were raised to its dead – its sagging belly was a bone-dump for the misguided; its underworld swallowed the vagrant, the junky, the man reaching to find another in the dark. I imagined the Queen of Hearts waiting at the entrance to the tunnel, making hair ribbons out of the scarlet thread which he would never dare employ in a journey to the interior. For a moment I considered creating a scandal for Father by going to live with the Queen of Hearts. The attraction of one man for another had already germinated inside me. What I had to clarify was my theoretical fear; the world had not prepared me for it. The excitement, the curiosity, the different orientation of my drive would result in a restricted but intensified milieu.

I opened the window to a scent of jasmine. I was thinking of the town's cholera victims, and of the Frenchman I had met who had been in quarantine on board a steamer anchored off Salto on the Banda Oriental bank of the Uruguay. He was a naturalist and was reading a green leather book with a gold spider embossed on the cover. He spoke of villages decimated inland, of the dead left unburied to be gutted by vultures, and of cattle driven delirious by the smell of blood.

Outside, a breeze was rustling the leathery fronds of a palm. I lay back contemplating what I knew I was leaving behind and imagining the still undefined territory I should come to explore. Europe still had the soft edges of a cloud, it was vague, floating, indistinct, a land mass that belonged to Monsieur Flammarion's historic reminiscences.

I remembered a ride last year on a day of excessive heat, when my horse almost by instinct pushed through a screen of ferns and bamboos to discover a stream. A huge tree with giant arums shaded the spot, white trumpet flowers drooping towards the water; and as the horse stooped to drink, it was as though I were being tilted towards the mirror in which creation was first reflected. I imagined the word generating the world in this fashion, projecting a geometrical infrastructure on the waters. I had strayed from the road and only the uneven jolting of my horse kept me from falling asleep in the saddle. Reality had become confused with dream so that I hung suspended in a heat haze. When I started to, all I could remember was the absolute lucidity of the stream. Everything else was blurred, imprecise, without substance. My body was saturated from incipient fever.

I continued at an easy somnambulistic rhythm before being

punched out of my stupor by an overpowering smell of decay. I was almost nose up to the decomposing body of a hanged man, his blotchy, discoloured corpse riddled by vermin, the ropy, sausage-coloured consistency of his flesh burrowed into by egg-laying parasites. I was cheek to cheek with a hatchet-faced privateer, his skin a livid pincushion of dotting flies. My horse reared, catapulting me into a bed of ferns. I got out from under and pushed through swathes of bushes, disturbing a floral snowstorm of saffron and purple butterflies, catching up with my horse again only after crossing the path of a giant, lozenged toad. Despite the nausea I felt I reproached myself with not returning to search the man's shredded jacket. A prospector, a deserter, a spy? – I should have liked out of morbid curiosity to have had some clue to his identity. Soon he would be a bleached skeleton hanging from a short-line of knotted hemp.

The rashered, eyeless face swam back to me, brutally aborted like that of the gibbeted figure in Baudelaire's poem 'Voyage à Cythère'. I had read the latter in a finely printed copy of *Les Fleurs du mal* which I had picked up from a visitor in Montevideo. Caution had me conceal it in a chest with my papers. I had heard through Monsieur Flammarion of the scandal surrounding the book and the author's being prosecuted for obscenity. Something inside me fattened like a grub on decay. I wanted to encounter rotting hulks of elephants, deserted cities with their dead left to blacken in the sun.

I drifted in and out of consciousness, listening for Alma's approach, expectant of her knock and dumb-eyed solicitations, hopeful that she would find me in my state of arousal, prepared, confident this time that I could control the indomitable sexual flood. The speed with which experience had overtaken my notions of fantasy and shattered the mirror in which I had been anticipating so many gradual arrivals had left me over-excited, nerves stimulated to the point of delirium. My skin crackled with electricity. Outside the window the sea was a blue blouse blown by the wind into lifting pleats. I imagined flotillas of blossom arriving from the islands, a solitary black swan on the wave transformed into an ebony goddess wading ashore to white coves untouched by human feet. Love and death and red poinsettias.

The air sensitised my skin, lay on it as though a swarm of migrating butterflies had chosen to cover my body as a place of rest. Antennae and feelers worked in like a series of dusting brushes, leaving a trace of gold powder. I could hear someone breathing on the other side of the door; a rhythm that volatilised my blood and had me come alive with throbbing urgency. An upwelling fire from the earth's core had rooted in my blood. Its ferocity had to be controlled, channelled, directed from a universal consumption to a particular attraction. In my heat I wanted to be bound in a sheath of tight black silk and rolled across a contrastingly cool surface, oiled until the sensation climbed out of me in constricted, fiery jabs, a chain of seed-pearls forming a molten insignia, an incandescent cooling.

In my anticipation big storms were rolling behind my eyes. Those sudden brown wind-clouds that blew from the Pampas, carrying off flat roofs, were driving in circles through my blood. I was too much for myself, a wheel that was straining at its circumference and threatening to break out of its circular design into another dimension. Faces were crowding in, unfocused, interchangeable fetishes; pouting red lips belled into a fuchsia bud and traced a red circle round the tip of my sex. The hallucination steadied – carnival faces swam through my room, orgiastic rites flickered behind my eyes. I lay back luxuriating in the expectation of Alma's rose-blown body.

When the knock came, her knuckles filmed in a handkerchief, I lay back anticipating her surprise at my closed eyes, my abandon, my partial nakedness, the movement of my hand which led the eye to my erection. I was conscious of nothing but the stream of my imagery, the erotic automata that lit up in my mind and whirled there with the intangible mobility of blue sunbeams.

The smell of the carnival was still on my skin, the acrid tang of saltpetre, the sour reek of sweat and smoke, and so too the visual stimulus of couples entwined on the grassland, in alleys, the Queen of Hearts's sexual heat as he lay outstretched on the bed, coaxing himself into the world of fantasy that preoccupied me now. I would experience Europe as a violent sensual dream. My sexual encounters conceived in a state of animated trance would never live to reproach me. In the sober light of day, sitting at the piano or at a desk, I would be dissociated from the weird geometry of my sex. Men, women, what did it matter? It was my partners who would suffer remorse, the blinding migraine that came with the white morning light flooding the room. And it was I who would wake and coldly write of my experiences with the objectivity of a detached spectator. I should be hunted through the underworld, the city's complex network of tunnels, underground passages.

The heat was diffusing through my body, working its way up from my scrotal base through the spine. I did not look up as I heard the door close quietly and someone enter the room. I tensed, waiting for the warmth of her body to find mine, the heavier contours to overlap my thinly defined edges. I knew she would roll on me before moving down to my waist, and that her movement would rock me like a skiff being boarded. When the contact came, it was without preliminaries or touch. I felt myself drawn into a silk oval, a tongue flicking my vein, working round to the head and drawing me deeper. The friction nettled me as though hot and cold snowflakes were alternately alighting on the outer skin, prickling there with the irritant of a feather tickling a foot. The cyclone was building in me, so that my head spun and the ungoverned sensation that seemed to be rooted somewhere in my depths started to assert a channellised focus, a slow mounting pressure, a spiral thread mounting in sensation, forcing a way up like an underground stream pushing towards the one fissure in the rock. My hands reached out instinctively to feel for shoulders, the concave slope of a spine, but the head remained pulled back, elusive of my grasp, inexorable in its rhythmic pattern. With the warm surf climbing to a crested wave, gaining in height as it ran for shore, I gave myself up to the force of its breaking. As I started to ejaculate, I felt I had connected directly with the sun. I strained towards a molten core, part of me contracting from the intensity, the other part exultant, overtaken, lifted up by the huge power.

I did not want to open my eyes. I was embarrassed by my singular gratification, and in the calm that flooded me I saw the wind-feathered green of the endless Pampas, and imagined horses, white horses lifting into the distance. I lay there, warm, relieved for a time of the animosity I felt for the world, the venom I should like to have stuck into Father's main line. When I opened my eyes there was no one. I could feel something abraiding my feet and sat up to find the sequined mask placed on the bed. It was watching me with the same contemptuous arrogance to which I had been subjected in that tiny room on carnival night. An exacting scrutiny I could not dissociate from the face I had briefly glimpsed, torn out of its mask and beaten savagely by armed police. A woman's, a man's, or something in between that had me think of a child with faun's ears and a libidinous mouth?

The voices were beginning again downstairs, one lagging behind the other, before their mutual uptake suggested a token agreement. I was waiting for the panic to set in, for the fear to grow huge in me at the realisation of what I had done. But nothing happened. I took off the mask and watched my numb, steely eyes register an assertive cold. Nothing appeared to have changed; clouds were still building out at sea and a fishing-boat scudded under sail for port. The universal cataclysm I expected to occur failed to take place. There was no branding of me with a scar or sign, a red Cain-mark by which my identity would be known. What alarmed me was the dexterity with which the Queen of Hearts appeared and disappeared. He might remain concealed in the house, and I should have to keep silent with my fear, so as not to create suspicion. I remembered his knife and the way the set of his eyes remained impassive, siphoning my life, reading me deeply as though he had contrived to look out of my eyes at himself seated on his bed. And if his voice started up in my head, I should be without defences. I began to imagine he would follow me to Tarbes and then to Paris. I should find him on the stair to my apartment or back to the wall at the end of an alley. I should be hunted across the face of the world. Sleepers would throw up their windows in country villages at the sound of my furious approach. And always I should be directed nowhere, my road an open-ended future.

I was suddenly cold. I waited for the slow delivery of blood to return and my unbending was like that of a tree righting itself after a persistent gale. I put on my clothes and returned to the window. The clouds had formed a solid indigo wad cratered by a white shell of light. The storm was going to miss us, it was being driven inland and would break over the Rio side of the estuary in vertical streamers of rain. Behind it travelled a blue clearing which would brighten to cerulean.

I knew as I sat there rafted on my bed, huddled into myself, that I was alone in life. Even my lessons had been abandoned, and instead of the increased study I expected to follow by way of punishment, it seemed that I was now to be shut up in my room and ignored. I decided to write my valediction to a country I knew I should never see again. Its white, rectilinear architecture, its cosmopolitanism, its steaming, choleric drains, its blue coasts and reeking abattoirs.

There was this boy – should I call him the Comte de Lautréamont? – who refused to leave a trace of himself outside of fiction. Everything he thought remained his because he left no identifiable clue by which it could be verified. In his birthplace he was without friends and almost without human contacts. He knew himself best in the aquarium proportions of the mirror in which he scrutinised his features to make sure no vestige of his inner life was portrayed in the face he presented to the world.

What came first was the sea and the rhythm of its ineluctable tides. It had gradually entered him, polished itself like a turquoise in his blood, and come to live in the pit of his belly. His spine was a sea snake evolving from that blue abyss. In fever he would hear a bell-buoy tinkling like a watchdog, or chimes from a drowned city rolling through the shoals of his hallucinated thought. The sea insulated and reminded him of the amniotic bubble in which he had lived as a foetus. A little crayfish alive in water. The force of that sea was responsible for his moods, his catatonic calm, the delirious frenzy of his ungovernable mania. When something or someone disturbed him, he felt as though a stone had plummeted into the glassiness of serene shallows. He would dive for that offending pebble, but gradually they accumulated to a bed of stones, too numerous and too individually heavy to retrieve from their place of deposit. His father's face, his mother's, his tutor's, all stared up at him from the strata into which they had sunk. At night he hunted those cobalt depths, armed with a diver's knife, but was chased away by the voracity of sharks. To go downwards was always a means of escape, the brilliant fauna contained parrot and humming-bird colours. He could open a window on a sea palace and live amongst turquoise mosaics. He was alone there.

The Comte de Lautréamont. How well the name had looked when first he had traced it out in the white sand of a cove! The name had come to him first through the novelist Eugène Sue, and he drew a circle round it as a kingdom and waited for the incoming tide to erase his secret. He had experienced a feeling of elation and complicity at the notion of an adopted pseudonym. When the surf found it, there was a glitter at first as though the letters had been illuminated, and finally the wave had hissed at his boots and flooded the signature. He ran up the beach, intoxicated by the prospect of his duality. In his mind he envisaged perpetrating crimes against humanity. He would watch the blood of the last man on earth drip into a glass and smash it. Only then would his desire to be alone find appeasement.

He had grown up without the capacity to love. His mother had promised him that in time his feelings would become polarised to someone, but the ice cutting him off would not thaw. She convinced him that what he felt for her was love, but in reality he knew it to be a means of siding against his draconian father.

He dreamt constantly of the power to be acquired by ceremonial magic, and of induction into the Cult of the Black Mother. He saw himself dressed in a white loincloth and led by four teachers to a small room where for sixteen days he would invoke spiritual insight into the meaning of the combination of male and female. He would go to Paris and study under the auspices of Eliphas Lévi. He had been lucky again, in that a French scholar staying at one of the hotels in Montevideo had loaned him one of Lévi's books. He liked too the idea that the occultist, after being expelled from his appointment at the Petit Séminaire de Paris, had found it necessary to adopt a new name. This had strengthened his own resolve to catch the world unawares by the anonymity of his arrival.

He would work by night and in secrecy, and watch the red dawn break over the roofs of the city. No one could know of the white honeycomb inside him, the cellular intricacy of a construction built out of inner light. In his imagination he envisaged an old vagrant climbing to his attic from the street. The man would bring hot bread with him, stolen from a doorstep, and they would exchange stories of the night over wine. In the conspiratorial quiet preceding the day they would sit like two men awaiting the dawn of a new age. No matter the ink and wine staining his sleeves, he was still the Comte de

Lautréamont, and his title granted him the authoritative power to confess a fictitious ancestry. And in the relating of who he was not, he would in turn be gaining new inroads into his own identity. Multipersoned, manipulative, protean, the self in living out fictions had still to return to its source before being recreated by the lie on the page.

Others would learn of his character as a free-thinker, as someone who reviled factions and class, a rebel in the cause of the imagination, a titled man who learnt of the Paris underworld from a coterie of vagrants, pimps and prostitutes. He would talk of the pursuits of those who aspired to knowledge of a psychosexual nature.

His listeners would include a priest whose apostasy had led to excommunication and a fanatical devotion to the black arts. Still carrying a mauve-plumed biretta, the man would punctuate his speech with Latinisms, his tiny, effeminate hands working to free his mind of some irritant, some sexual fantasy unappeased by even the most debased encounters in alleys. His hands would shake as an indication of the viral march of syphilis through his central nervous system.

What would become of those violet dawns and the cognoscenti after they had dispersed back to their solitary rooms? He saw himself sitting at a piano declaiming his sentences, accompanying his prosopopoeias by chords thumped out on the keys. It was a way of disordering and heightening the senses, his empty stomach on fire with the kick of red wine. Sometimes he would write on the mirror in coloured chalks, or lie down on the floor and dream of the life he had known in Montevideo. That had been lived by Isidore Ducasse, a relation of his with whom he was no longer on speaking terms. It was said that Isidore had left his red teeth-marks in his tutor's wrist after a disagreement over his lack of punctuality in attending classes, and that he had caught his father dressing Alma in his dead wife's silk lingerie and lashed him with a riding-crop. And it was rumoured that he prostituted himself in American hotels, waded up to his knees in the blood of cattle in municipal slaughterhouses, and mixed with butchers' sons, thieves, deserters, drug-pushers, and he DIDN'T CARE.

Ducasse had been the subject of controversies remembered to this day when Lautréamont sat destitute in his room fisting a piano to an insane dissonance.

He recalled the unpleasant incident of the dead cow, and how, when Ducasse had ridden out with a neighbour one Sunday in autumn to the small town of Las Piedras, to see Don Victor, a jaguar and puma hunter who lined his hut with their extravagant skins, he had already predicted the brutal incident which was to occur. Don Victor was drunk, and had insisted on blasting shot into a particularly valuable puma-skin he had stretched on the wall. Not content with peppering the skin with bullet-holes, he had smashed a bottle of whisky against his exhibit. Isidore wanted to see the man pinned up on the wall himself, and for a moment a blank spot had entered his consciousness, as though he had run out of a dark room into the light and was temporarily blinded. He had jolted out of it in time to be called to the yard to resaddle. His neighbour evidently did not trust the hunter's trigger-happy exuberance and thought it safer to head back. They took a dust road, glad to be clear of their manic acquaintance, and had ridden for only ten minutes before they were pulled up by the stench of rotting flesh. A cow had turned maggoty under a floripondio, the carrion black with insects and spading vultures. Disgusted by the nauseous smell, his neighbour was shocked to a halt to discover Isidore had dismounted and was testing the putrescent flanks of the cow with his boots, all the time clapping his hands and shaking with raucous laughter as the vultures flapped clear, their leathery wings beating the sapphire air. He had stood mesmerised by the energy attendant on decay, the breakdown of flesh by swarming parasites, and the breeding-ground it proved to be for an irascible drone of glinting flies. Unable to get close enough to the root of dissolution, he had taken hold of a log and laid into the gutted sores opened by vultures. Vermilion, purple, the fissures had fascinated, drawn him down to inspect the putrid lesions like one discovering the beauty of colour in a sea shell. It was only when he felt the cut of a whip behind his ears, and heard the enraged howl of his neighbour's voice shouting to him to get back to the road before he slashed his ears, that he had come back to himself and taken flight from the sun-cooked carcass. On their way back to Montevideo not a word was exchanged between the two riders – the incident was too disquieting for even Don Victor to report to Isidore's father.

There had been other things said of Isidore Ducasse. He was lazy and played bowls on a piece of waste land close to the harbour. He was obsessed with cock-fights and visited the harbour bars to watch two birds battling in a miniature Roman amphitheatre.

And what were his achievements, this blood dependant of the Comte de Lautréamont? He thought of the parasitical, awkward Isidore with disdain. He viewed the adumbrated highlights of that stranger's life with the clinical detachment necessary for art. He would spare only those features of a life that lent themselves to the elaboration of fiction. The rest would suffer an early and irretrievable dormition. This would be his most important task: the elimination of all personal facts that could not be assimilated into metaphor, and then the fragmentation of that metaphor into an impersonal mosaic. He would be helped in this by the knowledge that his father would almost certainly have destroyed his mother's papers after her suicide. And, given his own reputation, it was unlikely that a record would be kept of his past. He would also have to create an imaginary ongoing life for his father. Ends are like that; they cut you off from facts and necessitate the creation of a shadow life. Lautréamont would alter the balance of history by believing in nothing of the past. He believed in nothing but the truth established by the immediacy of metaphor. Everything else was to be mistrusted. His life suffered the exposure of a raindrop; but at the same time it had a blinding clarity of perception, a piercing scintillation that made it impossible for others to focus on without flinching.

Lautréamont would inherit Ducasse's determination to abolish rationalism and to detonate a literature entrenched in a doctrine of social realism. A link would be established between an umbrella and a sewing-machine, a red moon and a black sun setting above a pyramid. Lautréamont would open the floodgates of the unconscious, and the result would be the creation of new psychological states, patterns of behaviour that would configure in revolutions occurring on an inner plane, changes that would challenge man's whole concept of self-identity.

For years he had dreamt of uniting himself to his double. As he thought back in time he realised he had always been someone else, and that his energy had been concentrated into creating a dual figure. Only then had he realised that in time he would have to submit to the dominance of the superior power he had created.

The surf was slamming hard across the flat beach. Everything was caught up in the slide towards change – the molecular dance of the universe, the centuries disappearing into vortices the way pebbles rattled on the down gradient, to be caught up in the wave's retreating hem. And in the end there would be nothing but a heap of black pebbles on a white beach under a red sky. It was how he envisaged the end of the universe. And Lautréamont would witness the cataclysm. He would stand as the last man on a fire-scoured littoral, the big sheetings of flame burning to an emerald and black conflagration on the skyline.

It was not the coastline of Uruguay that met his vision, but the apocalyptic waste land he had prepared for the marriage with his double. A blue-eyed, lithic statuary followed him as he ran. The stone men who were waiting to come to life at a command. He was breathless, terrified to return to the unrelieved sterility of his home. Everything that had compromised his life now seemed immeasurably distant. The town appeared to have pushed off into mental space; he was separated from it by the gulf of a mental divide. He could never get back; he would need space and anonymity to give birth to Lautréamont. Somewhere a room awaited him in a European capital. Out of that window he would see the imperial eagle die in the hands of an inept emperor. The crowds were red ants running for crevices. The birth of the unknown hero always resulted in the collapse of civilisation. Lautréamont would have to be invincibly resilient to withstand the neglect that his work would suffer. There would not even be the friction aroused by hostility to mark the arrival of his genius.

The surf caught him again, but this time he made no effort to elude its blazing flood. He let it ride up to the level of his boots and continued to wade through the shallows, careless of his clothes, eyes fixed on an imperceptible point on the horizon. It was here in the Atlantic's turbulent energy, the ocean of his beginnings, that he would celebrate the union between himself and his double. A symbolic death followed by an instantaneous rebirth. He had brought the other this far, carried him through danger, nurtured his latent ambition, been unsparing in his preparations, and now all that remained was to concede his name and liberate the subject of his myth.

He watched a swallow dive to the beach. It was time for Lautréamont to emerge and live.

Part Two

Woodcut of Lautréamont by Méndez Magariños, after the photograph given to Alvaro Guillot-Muñoz by Eudoxie Ducasse

The Eye 6

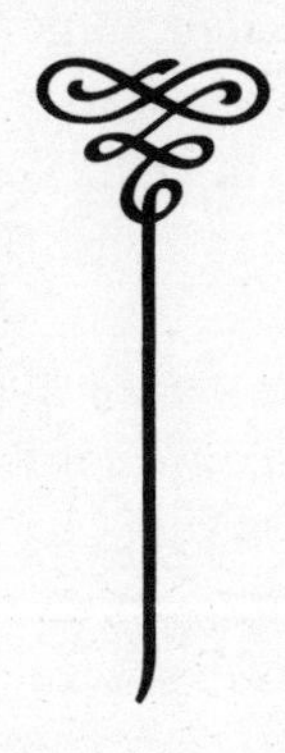

. . . I insist. I cannot provide you with duplicates of letters lost at sea. The irregularity of my reports from Tarbes and the greater consistency of letters reaching you from Paris suggest either interception or mismanagement in delivery. I incline towards the former.

You have surely received news of your son's unsavoury relationship with Paul Lespès and Georges Minvielle. I cannot repeat facts until I am sure that my letters reach you. In connection with the incident that occurred at school and Ducasse's imperious flaunting of authority, I am surprised you have not heard from Gustave Hinstin. The latter must have written to you in confidence about your son's moody and unpredictable behaviour?

What I know of Ducasse's life in Paris comes from Marthe David, a prostitute resident at 45 rue Barbesse. She knows him under the adopted name I have communicated in an earlier letter. Her presentation of him agrees neither with yours nor mine. She speaks of him as a young man who belongs to a secret order whose aim is to establish universal power. It is difficult to ascertain whether she has in mind a political body – the revolutionary spirit is rife in Paris – or one of the esoteric lodges. Her inarticulacy and general evasiveness on all matters relating to her life do little to assist my research into your son's equally enigmatic life.

What I can establish is a certain predictability in your son's habits. His behaviour here differs little from his preoccupations in Montevideo. He spends most of his time alone, seems to avoid friendships, takes pains on leaving his room to conceal his papers, and on going out shows an indifference to street life. What happens in his life seems to come about by chance. His few excursions, which have taken in the Roman amphitheatre in the rue Monge, the ruins of the Cluny baths and two visits to see the *Venus de Milo* in the Louvre, are done with a nonchalance that suggests a disdain for his physical surroundings.

His activities seem to be confined to his room at night. He writes, plays the piano and on occasions entertains the sort of man to whom he was attracted in Montevideo. Only these are different; they resemble vagrants, nocturnal revenants. I can establish no trace of a political movement and as yet nothing in his behaviour likely to create the sort of scandal that would threaten your position.

The books he buys are largely related to natural history. He seems fascinated by their plates and is selective in his choice of editions.

I shall await your further instructions, which will in turn be a confirmation that my letter has reached you.

Chapter 6

Twenty-three rue Notre Dame des Victoires. An address and a room in which to write. My skyline is dominated by the Haussmannisation of Paris – the network of elevated scaffolding that correspondingly plunges the Government into massive debt. I can hear the chain-gangs of workers trooping to the sites at first light. All day the thunder of falling masonry, the big flash that brings a block down like a house of cards. On frosty days the metallic ring of hammers, the industry of a pick-axe alerts each nerve in my body like a wire. Smoke billows from the site and anchors in the sky as a black willow before drifting off across the Bousse.

What I miss is the steady beat of metronomic surf. Those lapis lazuli and malachite depths in the wave as it rises to take on the colour of the sky before slanting into a white incline.

Paris affords me the isolation I had hoped to find. I sleep in the day and work at night. My friends are those who walk the city at night, those who are placated by the conspiratorial quiet, those for whom the darkness is a shell that hums with the reciprocal echo of their inner dictates. I gained nothing by my education: what I have, what I know, has come to me through the union between silence and apprehensible vision.

When I came to France, first as a boarder at the Lycée Impérial of Tarbes and later as a pupil of a school in Pau, my nerves revolted against my physical and mental displacement. I withdrew. I studied Latin prose and grammar, not with the relish of a classical scholar but with the mind of one intent on studying magic and on following a precise discipline in order to train my senses for the universal disorder I should come to create. Tarbes turned out to be every bit as provincially delimiting and disciplinarian as Flammarion had impressed on me. A town with a convent, a cathedral, its leisurely bells invading the silence with a deadening, oppressive inertia; the chilblains, the mortuary cold of the dormitories, the brutality that existed between pupils, the medicinal smells of the infirmary, the fresh-bread smell of the linen-room. Elbows on the desk, my head in my hands, I sat staring at a textbook without reading it. I dreamt of freedom; azure skies blowing above banana trees, green bee-eaters chasing dragonflies, the wind in tall grasses. I had to prove myself to the youth I had left behind – Isidore Ducasse. I even took to penning him long letters, and prided myself on concealing my identity from the two persons with whom I shared not so much a friendship as a tenuous acquaintance. Paul Lespès and Georges Minvielle. How little they knew of me. And how unimportantly morose they seem to me now – they whose ambitions amounted to nothing more than the expectation of minor employment.

I used to go out with them to a willow-ringed pool where we bathed in summer. The willow crowns sat in the lacquered pond like green haystacks. We could hear toads bubbling in the grasses, a magpie rattling in a poplar. They were retarded and could think of nothing but parodying the eccentricities of our teachers, and adopting the bravura of young men who had experienced their first red-headed provincial prostitute. We would lie back in the grass and smoke, I remaining silent, while they exaggerated their repertoire of obscenities.

For I long time I tolerated their asinine obtusity – turtles sunning on the bank, their attempts to prove amphibious failing even after repeated efforts to acclimatise to the cool water. I wanted to shock them, to prove to them that I was not a part of their world of Latin cramming, Horatian odes, all the tedious effluvia that snaked downstream into a ministry's deposit pool.

I waited my time. After the long, intolerable boredom of staying on at Tarbes during the ravaging dog days of the summer vacation, we met on a warm day in September, when the chestnut leaves were yellowing and Lespès and Minvielle had returned from the long break at their respective homes. Minvielle was boasting how he used to take a local girl into the hayloft, and how, as an added delectation to their pleasure, she would flick her tongue tantalisingly over his erection, before alternately contracting and dilating on the head, coaxing him to orgasm. I could tell he was lying by the awkwardness of his narration, and that his desire remained unrealised, a fantasy he was too shy to take to a brothel. Their conspiratorial tone was designed to exclude me from the conversation. I could feel my blood freeze as though I were suddenly immersed in cold water. Without giving the least hint of my intentions I fell on Minvielle, pinning him down in the grass, while his friend, terrified by my white temper, backed off, unwilling to risk inviting my aggression.

I wanted to prove him a liar, humiliate him before his friend, so my right hand forced his trousers open, and all the while I kept spitting into his ear, 'This is really what you like, isn't it?', feeling his spontaneous erection grow in my hand, his involuntary arousal stimulated by our body-to-body tussle in the grass, my stronger hold keeping him captive beneath me, his confusion and fear showing in his dilated eyes, his attempted resistance overpowered by the animal instinct that was stronger even than his sense of shame. His companion remained rooted to the spot. My quick backward glance found him fish-mouthed, white, his whole sensibility trying to blank out the reality that was happening before his eyes.

'This is what you really like, isn't it, Minvielle?' I shouted as I got up and left him in a state of exposure. I stormed off, tucking my clothes in as I went, dusting my black trousers, and leaving the two to resolve an issue that neither could transpose into a joke.

The occasion ws never mentioned again. After that I became more solitary, more withdrawn, my hauteur commanding not contempt but respect. I was seen as an unmanageable foreigner, someone unlikely to be interested in the commonplace pursuits of my fellow-boarders. Left alone I had to compensate by indulging my imagination. My visions were intense, luminous, apocalyptic, but I was always in control of them, turning them outwards and away from madness, despotic in my subjugation of a world conceived imaginatively. If I had politicised my views, armies would have assembled in the name of my manifestos, troops would have marched in obedience to the angel of revelation, my book in their hands, the black clouds building over Europe, a dense cumulus shattered by red fire.

My precociousness, my failure to subscribe to orthodoxy, led to an eventual confrontation with my teacher, Gustave Hinstin. After I had repeatedly refused to eliminate the imagery from my essays, I was dragged out in front of the class to have the offending passages ridiculed in public. He had hoped to make of me a fishmonger's exhibit, the tail-stiffened, red-mouthed *nature morte* of a fish stored under ice. Instead I relished the ignominy attendant on my person, the ridicule intended to reduce me to a scapegoat in the eyes of a class suddenly collected around its teacher. But I was impervious to the eyes coming at my face. I recognised in my rhetoric the impoverished mediocrity of my detractor. He would live his life under the delusion that poetry was marble chipped from the classics, a bloodless monument immune to a transfusion from the street, a shock injection imploding the unconscious. As he read out my imaginative flights with deprecating emphasis on metaphor, I felt uplifted, as though I were staring into the blue eye of a future invisible to my contemporaries.

When Hinstin stopped reading, his face was white with rage. His silent admonition warned me to get out and stay out. My retreat was leisurely. I savoured the incomprehension on the moon-faces that turned all the way round to watch me go. Horse-flies spotted the air outside. I spat and walked out to the willow-ringed pond.

My convictions have not altered; they have deepened in accordance with my isolation. In a city you live like an eagle in its eyrie up above it all, or else succumb to the levelling criterion of the masses. From the vantage-point of my attic, I am conscious of what it is to live nearer the sky. The cloud changes are continuous; great continents of white cumulus build into vaporous ranges, and are as suddenly blown away to reveal an azure cube. One is closer to the quiet lexicon of night rain falling on the slates, to the spitting crackle of hail and the big concourse of winds tugging at verticals. I work through those changes which wash or stain my page.

At first I used to write cursory notes to my father, explaining nothing of my way of life, for fear of further earning his displeasure, but always swinging a plumb-line into his financial reserves. My requests for money were seldom met. Like all weak men my father lived his life without consideration for others. His physical unattractiveness encouraged him in even more marital infidelities, for, being unconscious of his own appearance, he attached little importance to the beauty of others.

My letters from Monsieur Flammarion were of a different nature and invited a reciprocal intrigue in the politics of the day. He feared the Republic's increased power and the depositional threat it constituted to Napoleon III. His tone was one that made it clear that I would be suitably recompensed if I chose to work as a spy and supply his party with the information necessary to apprehend revolutionaries. His letters also intimated that if he visited Paris he would be pleased to see me, but what I read into the nature of his suggestions was sexual. There was that ambiguity, neither stated nor concealed, which implied a liaison of a nature he had clearly contemplated for a long time and hoped to consummate.

At first I considered taking him up on his intentions. The sadist in me would have delighted in ruining him, in exposing him in public, so that he would be arrested in a sordid alley close to the river.

Unable to extricate myself from the intricacy of his web, I fed him with small details. My pretended sympathies were spurious. It mattered little to me whether Charles Floquet spat in the Tsar's face 'Long live Poland!' or whether Napoleon was nursing a hernia, gonorrhoea or congested kidneys. I had to return home that summer and hoped to extort from Flammarion the funds that my father consistently denied me.

My brief return had been a mistake from the beginning. Mountainous green seas had pursued us across the Atlantic, whitecaps churned up in the wake of a hurricane broke over the poop, smashed across mid-decks and had the boat climb almost vertical before being dropped into a corresponding depression. When the wind abated, fog became our new adversary. We drifted through a dense white sea-smoke, fearing at any moment that a ship would run us down.

We went ashore once to replenish our water supplies and came to a beach where three wrecked vessels had foundered. Two of them were lying on their beam-ends, surf-smashed, and the third, a flat-bottomed vessel, sat bolt upright on an even keel much further inshore than the other two. The shore was scattered with a mosaic of debris and wreckage, washed up in long spits, junked together and heaped into beached tumuli by the devastating assault of breakers. There were empty cigar-boxes, a case of surgical instruments, another of artificial limbs and an overspilled chest of dolls, clown-faced toys with their glued-on black or yellow hair, matted by the salt, and close to them a drowned man was rolling about in the surf, his body wedged between rocks, the face disfigured, nose and ears gone, the skin razor-slashed into pulped welts by the cutting edge of jagged stones.

The site appeared to have escaped the attention of looters. A little further on I discovered a broken case of champagne, in which there were a few unopened bottles. I released a cork and almost choked on the lively kick of foam. My head blew. It seemed to be detaching itself from my body and kiting up on a vertical axis. Other bodies in various states of decomposition littered the frothing shallows. One was headless, another showed a caved-in chest, truncated arms and legs, suggesting a clean scythe-cut by a shark's mouth. Suddenly I was thrashing out into the water, breaking the surf with my knees, fascinated by the gaping red hole in the side of a body impaled on a submerged rock. The shallows were jumping with blazing fauna, crazy reds and marigolds and violets were sluiced into rotating whorls.

Something lit up in my brain. I felt that same sense of reckless exhilaration as I had on the occasion when I had laid into the rotting cow blackened by vultures. I grappled the body off the impaling needle and dragged it towards me. I held the blotched corpse in my arms, pushing it from side to side as though caught up in an aquatic dance. The cavity was gaping, raw, a pulp of disintegrating tissue, but the colour seemed to me to resemble an underwater sun, a red disc that rose daily over the fish-thronged architecture of Atlantis. I pulled the body upright and rested it against my chest for support. The face had no eyes, ears or nose. I tilted it back, then swung it round in a half-circle before smashing it on to its back at the wave's edge. The surf licked at it on the outgoing wave before cleansing it on the run-in. It was like a purifying rite, seeing the surf steam over that red hole. I waited for the outwash to retreat, took one last look at the squid-bloated body, slatted with blue serrations, and made my way back towards the mass of wreckage. My manic overreach had given rise to depression, and I sat down on a beer crate and looked out to sea. The world was like that, there was either too much or too little of it. The stench, the stacked flotsam, the impurities that runnelled across the beach, all of these things had become odious. I remained rooted. I could smell a storm building out at sea. Clouds would suddenly be shaken like a lilac bush into a mass of whipped purples.

It was only when a skiff came in close to my part of the shore, on a last-minute reconnaissance, that I ran out through the shallows, waving my arms to attract attention, and I was then bundled into the boat and rowed out to the *Cythera*.

At home I was greeted with the indifference accorded a stranger. My father had been promoted again and spent much of his life at social functions, his weight increasing with his sense of self-importance. Flammarion was still in daily attendance and manifested an unconcealed power over him. It was he who moved through the house as if it were his own, and he who dictated the laws of conversation at the dinner-table. His thin, effete fingers were suddenly a lobster's pincered claws snapping tight on each exposed nerve-end.

What occurred was the inevitable conflagration between Father and myself. It turned out that he had paid to have me followed and knew of my attraction to prostitutes in the ninth arrondissement. His informant had given him the name of Marthe David, a red-haired girl, profusely tattooed with green and blue snakes on arms she deliberately exposed. He knew that Marthe lived at 45 rue Barbesse, behind closed shutters. What shocked me more was his discovery that I went under the name of Lautréamont in Paris.

I listened to his anger ricochet from wall to wall. The echo returned with the deadness of a lead ball dropped into a well. I was to be construed as a parasite, a drug addict who would rot of syphilis. Despite his claims to the contrary, Father was becoming rich. I had heard from a street acquaintance that he had bought the Hôtel des Pyramides, where he entertained ballet dancers with champagne. What I had pieced together of Father's behaviour over the years all pointed to a way of life which excluded my mother. His taurine masculinity, obsessive career drive and the coarseness of his sexual preferences had never been concealed in deference to her sensitive nature. On the contrary they had been flaunted as though he were punishing Mother for making any marital claims on him. She was the psychological anchor that had dragged at his crowded sails on the high seas of worldly ambition.

'You will amend your ways,' he shrieked, 'or be thrown out of this house and the shelter afforded by my name. And let this be my last word to you: your lusts will be your ruin. When you're running with sores, you'll be left to die in the gutter. Now get out!'

When the door slammed as though blown behind me by a great wind, I stopped and listened to myself think. I could hear the stream of my thoughts. Everything I had not said had been stored in a silent dialogue and was seeking a rapid release. I should like to have accused him of murdering Mother and to have her body swim up from the night waters of his unconscious. I wanted to tell him that Marthe specialised in O and A and that the lingam and yoni were tattooed on her bottom in red and indigo.

I found calm in looking out of the window at the turquoise arch of the sky. Scarlet passion-flowers and orange begonias created a sun-storm in the garden. Everything went on living independent of man, uncontained by his consciousness, restrained by its cyclic limitations, the duration of its season. As I stood there, I felt a hand rest on my shoulder. The lightness of touch was accompanied by the resolution not to let go. The hand was weighted with a purpose guided by thought and not physical strength. I knew without turning round that it was Monsieur Flammarion's. I remained motionless.

'Someone's been looking for you,' he said, with a note of conspiracy in his voice that I had for long suspected but never heard. 'He comes from a poor quarter of the town, a person your father would have locked up if he knew of his visiting the house. He wouldn't leave a name but said you could find him out on the coast.'

The subtle emphasis the voice laid on the latter directive was sufficient to inform me of the equally ambivalent choice implied by his raising the subject.

'It's my duty to speak of this in order to spare your father further suffering,' he said, resuming the persuasive tone he had once employed as my tutor. 'If you wish to speak to me about it, you will find me in your father's library.'

My only thought was to get back to Paris and secure sufficient funds from Father to make my life there seem practicable. The facts surrounding Mother's death would serve as a point of conscience, a picklock's probe into the recess where his guilt burned with a bright flame. He must have tried so often to extinguish the fire, got up at night thinking the house was burning down, and found that the conflagration was alive in his head.

I had resolved to stay no more than a week. I could find no vestige of the reality that I had lived here at some stage in my life. At night I bolted the shutters, for I knew the Queen of Hearts would be watching the house. Father's unrelieved insomnia and his insistence in keeping the house lights on, so that he could walk around at will at night, were an additional protective to my sleepless nights. I could hear Father pacing the library before he unlocked the bedroom that Mother had occupied and went in. He stayed a long time unlocking drawers, before reappearing with his leg audibly dragging in the corridor. If I had looked out then I should have seen him age twenty years in the distance between his own and Mother's bedroom. He was like a man attempting to carry his own weight in his arms, save that the volume increased with each step.

Alma kept away from me. It was clear she had become Father's mistress, and paradoxically his slave. Even her method of speech had changed, and her once spontaneous exuberance had been replaced by an awkward consideration of words. She reminded me of the catatonic wall-blank stare of madmen I had seen in the streets of Paris. Men who shuffled through the night in rags, their eyes preoccupied with an inner reality that stopped so far short of externalising it seemed they would never connect with the immediacy of things.

It was the familiar rhythm of surf that restored me. Its voluble thunder hung in the air, turning the bowl of the sky into an echo-chamber. In Paris that same music lived with me, only it was internalised, the clap of dice in a cup, the audio-stimulation of memory. A few unmoving clouds stayed dead on the horizon; they were like white dabs of paint fixed there by brush-strokes.

In the same way as I had removed myself from my birthright by adopting the name of Lautréamont, so I conceived of further distancing myself by creating *Les Chants de Maldoror*. Maldoror would be the perpetrator of crimes imagined by Lautréamont. My disguise would be made invincible by the creation of a third party. Maldoror's black lyricism would remain an unquantifiable enigma to the epoch in which he lived. His poetry would disorder the nerves like the atonal dissonant music I improvised at the piano.

Maldoror would be the oracular scapegoat whose voice belonged to no time in his anticipation of final things. In preparation for his embodiment, I had already written of him: 'I received life like a wound, and I have forbidden suicide to heal the scar. I want the Creator – every hour of his eternity – to contemplate its gaping crevasse. This is the punishment I inflict on him.'

Left alone I kept to my room or wandered upstairs to the attics. I had grown accustomed to my enforced isolation in Paris, and here the house I knew was lodged on the sea-floor, its windows open to the drowned.

Since our brief encounter, Monsieur Flammarion had made himself inaccessible. He had grown into the unauthorised master of a house he had come to dominate. Whatever it was he had observed in Father, and by slow degrees opened up like a seam, stitch by unravelled stitch, had begun long before Mother's death. If I listened hard enough I could believe I heard the almost imperceptible beat of his eyelids as he read. His concentration was that of someone who read in order to focus his mind on a larger problem. I thought of how little I knew of this man outside his routine life in our house. It had never occurred to me to find out where he lived and with whom, and why he should always be available to Father.

That my movements in Paris had been followed seemed more in line with Monsieur Flammarion's way of thinking than Father's. As the author of such a scheme his cunning would be vulpine, his assessment of the written reports offered, meticulous. I was biding my time, filling in the plot piece by piece, and learning to think as he did, by listening.

At night there were the customary fireworks, and the lighthouse's garnet eye fixed on the coastal waters. This was the time I came alive, my imagination dragging up images from the unconscious. Maldoror lived as the recurrent end and beginning, the black serpent swallowing its tail. It was then I would begin writing, and in my overreach into the psyche I tapped resources that grew into an autonomous fiction.

In the quiet of the noon a single man entered a deserted village. His footsteps echoed in the square and came back at him as a series of reproaches. The deep well had been quicklimed, the animals slaughtered. The man entered house after house, his tall figure ducking beneath the low doorways, his loping stride eating up the earth. He came to a whitewashed wall on which someone had written in blood: THE SHADOW LIVES ON THE INSIDE. WE SAW NOTHING.

He dismissed the sign and kept on in his search. Once when a mirror gave back his reflection he smashed it, for he did not recognise what he saw. When he came to the last house, which gave on to the slopes of scorched foothills, he set fire to it, not knowing that the one surviving human lay on a mattress inside, waiting only to confide the universal secret of good and evil to the person she had heard coming up from the valley. That man was Maldoror.

Sometimes the dawn would find me still up, exhausted from having lived through a night of generation and death. Already my creation had come to assert an independent orbit around an unsetting inner sun.

I would dress and, white-faced, go down to breakfast, anxious to dispense with the formality so that I could sleep through to the early afternoon. Monsieur Flammarion would enter the room soon after Father and the talk would centre upon the *mazorca* – the Mafia who served under Rosas's dictatorship and whose methods of extortion were a constant source of fear to the inhabitants of Montevideo. Only last week they had set fire to a cattle ranch by making a human torch of its owner and spurring his tarred figure into a hayloft. People feared these terrorists. They descended on farms like a black thundercloud riding out of the sun.

The faint air of disquiet that Father manifested in Flammarion's company was evident on the morning that put an end to my brief stay. I had sensed the seam in Father's thinking at the breakfast table. It was like a black line drawn across a white cloth. The hinge in his thought would not close. It flickered, lending him an air of distraction.

When I went into his study I was aware of the sudden space that opened up in Monsieur Flammarion's absence. There was more light and air in the room. Father appeared larger, more focused, and anxious to hold centre stage. He puffed himself up in order to give voice to his authoritarianism, but there was a perceptible slackening in his rigidity. Suddenly he relaxed his taut shoulders and sat down. He faced the papers spread on his desk and, looking down, said: 'For reasons that are no concern of yours, I have dismissed Monsieur Flammarion from the household. As for your affairs, with which I cannot bring myself to sympathise until you pursue a regular profession, I have entrusted a solicitor with a small annuity to be made payable to you so long as you amend your behaviour.'

As I stood in his study for what I knew would be the last time, and smelt the beeswax polish which Alma so assiduously worked into the oppressive mahogany furniture, I tried to envisage Monsieur Flammarion caught scrutinising Father's private correspondence; his quizzical eyebrows arched as he discovered a potentially incriminating sentence. Or was it the other way round? I wondered. Could it have been Flammarion who had confronted Father with some aberration of conduct, and as a consequence been dismissed for his audacity?

After a pause, Father nodded as an indication that I should leave. A blue light was flooding the rectangular window. Even today that azure frame represents my inner perspective when I look out over the city's roof-tops, and it goes on multiplying itself to infinity.

The Eye 7

Your confirmation reassures me. Gustave Flammarion's dismissal from your service should make for an uninterrupted flow of mail. The psychological repercussions of his removal will inevitably be reflected in your son's behaviour.

I wonder too how long it is safe for me to stay on here. The times are bad and the mob may rise. Your son remains confined to his room. There is a light on at all hours. What little I have managed to read of his writings is to me incomprehensible. Marthe David retrieved a number of pages from his waste-paper basket which were intended for burning. I pieced together as best I could an almost indecipherable script. Nothing made sense. I feared at first that Isidore Ducasse is mad and is devoted to nothing else but the commitment of his dementia to paper. But on reflection it occurred to me that these writings may comprise a code – Masonic, hermetic, esoteric. How else explain the lines: 'Who is opening the door of my funeral chamber? I had said no one was to enter. Whoever you are, get out; but if you have convinced yourself that there is a mark of suffering or fear on my hyena's face.... He wanted to prove himself the universal monarch....'

The sheets are badly torn and my quotations approximate, but I imagine that the themes are consistent throughout his writings. I am constantly faced by the difficulty that your son has people visit him. He never risks fear of detection by going to places that might incriminate him.

Sometimes he visits the rue Vivienne; but again to no purpose. There is a barricade at the end of this street and a building site. Your son has always been attracted to such places. He stares at the fire which the workmen keep burning on the site, but meets no one. I have asked in the adjoining shops and cafés, but he meets no one there and neither collects nor leaves letters. I intend to pursue this line of interest further.

When and what he eats remain a mystery. To the best of my knowledge he lives on bread and wine. He visits a wine-seller and buys good Bordeaux reds. This and books seem to be his main source of expenditure.

His bookseller divulges nothing. A small, olive-headed man in a red fez who goes by what I suspect to be the adopted name of Henri Lorrain, and whose shop is at pont Marie, is by all accounts a radical propagandist. Meetings are held in his cellar, which contains a printing press. There is no evidence that Isidore Ducasse has political associations with the man, but undoubtedly they share a common link.

I await your further instructions. In the case of revolution, Ducasse will certainly take ship home and I shall follow in his wake.

Chapter 7

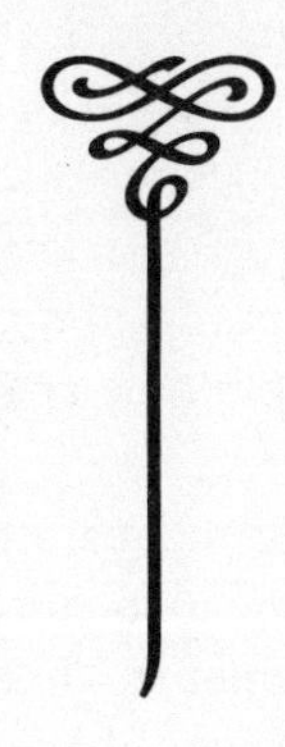

Thirty-two rue du Faubourg Montmartre. A change of address but not of habits. I still live on the top floor, my all-night light attracting the curious and those who maintain a conviction to live on the edge.

I live in fear of my work being discovered and burnt. A cursory police raid would result in the liquidation of my papers or an appearance before the Court of Cassation, which sits in a darkened courtroom and whose prevailing climate is to legislate against literature which in any way attempts to undermine the Bonapartist regime.

They have cost me my health, these interminable red dawns in which *Maldoror* has been conceived: this other through whom I celebrate poetic vision in the face of political factions, crowd riots, the momentum of a century bursting its floodgates.

My window turns from green to blue; the morning star twinkles above the Seine. At this hour the big contentions occur on an inner plane – madness is the bull that is led to the slaughter, head down, nostrils flaring, the wild pitch of its horns resisting captivity. When it charges across the page, words fly upwards, terrorised by its black, thundering hoofs. I have nothing but a hand with which to restrain this bolt.

The biography of a poet is written on the inside. My days correspond to those of my fiction, and there is little overlap left in which to pursue the autonomous drift chronologised by literary historians. I keep my duality secret; in that way no one can slip between it and me.

If I try to imagine how my acquaintances see me, then it must be as someone whose independence is suspect despite his revolutionary pronouncements. I maintain an impeccable appearance: white linen shirts, black velvet suits, the casual floppiness of a red silk bow. My books and piano profess my interests to the discriminating, but there is no real clue to my identity here, for I keep no papers other than my immediate writings and destroy all correspondence that comes to me either from Montevideo or Paris. Baudelaire's publisher, Poulet Malassis, writes to me from Brussels, warning me of the risk involved in publishing my book, and I memorise his letter before burning it. I recall his words on those nights when the work is with me like a fire lit in the hills: 'Your aesthetic expression of evil implies the most vital appreciation of good, the highest morality. In this you inherit the tradition of the modern sensibility begun by Flaubert and Baudelaire in their recognition of the interplay between good and evil in man.'

I try to imagine this man, his hands stained with printer's ink, his eyes myopic from reading galleys, his unfailing humour disarming his creditors. I think of him as preoccupied with the weight, the watermark and the grain of handmade papers, and in the selection of a type-face which will sit slightly raised on the paper, permanent in its execution.

Maldoror's raging pace will electrify the uninitiated. They will read it, as it was written, by night, their ears finding in its music the beat of a new age. I cling to the likelihood of its publication. I who have buried my name, hidden my life, concealed my person, take a delight in the confusion that such a book will cause. Its passage will be slow, its journey a long one, its bite like that of fire consuming a hayfield.

I avoid the literati and their cognoscenti: those who compensate for lack of originality by the acquisition of power. Lacroix calls on me sometimes and asks to read whatever new work I have done on *Maldoror*, but invariably I plead that it is still incomplete, thereby keeping the text to myself. It is arranged that the first canto will appear in an anthology called *Parfums de l'âme*, to be published in Bordeaux.

On the few occasions that I have ventured into the company of men who write, I have been disappointed. I have heard their names – the flaking stucco of the lionised demigods – Gautier, the younger Dumas, the bitingly mordant Goncourt brothers, Renan, George Sand, the ageing, choleric and vicious Sainte-Beuve, the gallery of those who thought the march of their words would alter the world only to find that their books had predeceased them.

These occasions rarely differ. A fourth-floor flat in the rue Vaneau, furnished in red plush with portraits by Ary Scheffer on the walls, the conversation shifting from political contention to attacks on the Academy, and then the party's dispersal to a red-light district, with one woman in attendance, a *décolletée* blonde who claims never to have removed the red rose Manet painted on her spine, and demands that she be allowed to use a spy-hole to watch one of the more bizarre fetishes.

But mostly I am alone. Memories assemble like that – a lifetime is built out of associations that belonged to a moment. A blue bay remembered at a time of flowering mimosa, a face with red lips and a gold earring seen through mist on an autumn boulevard. The endless fictions multiply. It is when words vibrate on those nerve-endings that the crystallised image is conceived.

What appears most disquieting to me in isolation is the dilemma of how to use time. There is either too much or too little of it; we either live inside, painfully contracting horizons, or feel ourselves isolated in the vastness of space. I seem to have lived with the palm of my hand balanced on the tip of a knife, writing what in theory I would call the Preface to a Future Book. And the relation of time to creation should always appear like that, a ratio that describes the fullness of energy brought to a particular stage of one's life, so that each work is a preface to a stage at which one has still to arrive, the logical extension of which is death.

I live for the blaze of metaphor that unites incongruities. The red wine-stain on my page is like an intoxicant to the dance of words. It is a little ritual I undertake, this sprinkling of wine-spots on the paper.

A day, an hour, a month, they are much alike – words twinkling like drops of lit oil, sometimes refusing to settle, others cut like black marble into an assumed permanence. Those who call on me do so to drink and talk of the wrong in their lives and how it stays there like a bruise in an apple. These men are diverse, monomaniacal, at odds with the age. One fears he has committed the murder of which he dreamt, believing he disposed of a man in the Seine, and that if he sleeps, the man's eyes will open inside his head.

And in my own way I have come to realise in exploding the imagination that man is without mental healers. The implosive visions I channel into *Maldoror* feed on the same potential that fuels the odd who are attracted to me. They know nothing of my writings, except where my speech betrays a preoccupation with the concerns of my poem. These night conversations up above the city are a means of isolating the present, stepping off a moving train and believing that one has succeeded in slowing down time by the fact that one is walking while the train is accelerating towards Moscow.

I have no regrets for the Ducasse I buried in South America.

He would have stayed and eventually conformed. If I were still him, I should be sitting in a cool government office, exercising a cigar-cutter on the tip of a seasoned Havana and discussing administrative means of controlling revolutionary outbreaks.

Here they speak of the Prussian coalition and of Napoleon invading Bismarck's Prussia with the assistance of Austria. And in Paris the anti-dynastic factions riot, loot jewellers and furriers and make love in the streets. The same power that drives my unconscious is pushing men forward like arsonists converging on the Tuileries. Unrest is undermining the city's equilibrium. The Republican fanatic who comes to my room speaks of the Emperor's ill-health, and how he has aged twenty years in three months. The Empire is on a crash course to extinction.

For the first time the sound of men running through the street late at night, or the sudden discharge of explosives somewhere in the city, had me sit up startled. My attention had been drawn to something I had not realised existed because I had no need to take it seriously. I found myself going down to the street at dawn and scooping up handfuls of the badly printed broadsheets that littered the gutters. Propagandist mendacities, they were nevertheless tangible evidence of a real dissatisfaction with Napoleon and his immediate circle. Rain-blotched, vehement caricatures, riddled with printer's errors and spelling mistakes. I gathered them up and took a childish delight in their crudities. They were like multicoloured autumn leaves wedged into drifts and pulped by the rain, the incessant trampling of feet.

Other, bigger storms preoccupied me. My always delicate health was beginning to show evidence of being stretched. For several days I locked my door and lay in the darkness, hearing a black surf roar through my veins.

I began to visit Marthe David again, taking a perverse delight in the knowledge that I was followed. I liked to watch Marthe brush out the red storm in her hair. It was like a field of poppies: a sunset that fell just short of her waist. She would playfully imitate a tiger, padding around the room on all fours, bottom up, inviting me to rush her from behind. Marthe in her elbow-length leather gloves and a face-net spotted with sequins: she would sugar me and peck at the tip like a strawberry.

Her naïve, childlike imaginings were in distinct contrast to the avarice she displayed for money. She would speak of her childhood in Rouen while painting a nipple, and of her father who had run off one summer night. This bricky, squat-shouldered man, who was of Russian descent, was a signalman on the provincial track. He had gone off with a local farm girl, while Marthe's mother shouted across the fields at nightfall. She waded out barefoot across streams, beat on doors, searched through barns and outhouses, frightened nervous horses in their stables and came home distraught, exhausted.

Marthe remembered it all with an exactness of detail which was terrifying. Her nerves cried out to embody the experience in a creative form, but all she knew was the allure of her body to men, the sale of her flesh for whatever price she could exact.

Marthe, whose particular speciality was protracted fellatio, recollected other childhood experiences. The brown-eyed cattle with their smoking breath in the autumn meadows bright with yellow oak leaves, the provincialism of the farmers, who spoke of nothing but their herds, the failure of their crops, hail damage to their blossom, the low price received for selling a calf to slaughter.

When Marthe told of these things her face softened before she checked it and hardened herself against any show of emotion. She had found respite from stress in painting water-colours, small village scenes in primary blues, yellows, greens, until one day the concrete disappeared and in its place she had painted abstract configurations to depict an unpeopled field with a thunderstorm building above the meadow. She had gone on doing this until one day the power was no longer with her and there was nothing to paint. She did not know why or where it had gone, only that its disappearance coincided with the beginnings of her menstrual cycle. There was nothing to paint and her moodiness had her fight with her mother and go off for long walks by herself, looking for something she knew was not there.

Instead she took to painting her eyes black and her mouth red, and at first people laughed at the child's precocity, the facetiousness of a schoolgirl emulating an artist's model. She grew to be a symbolic representation of what the men in her village most desired yet feared to touch, until one day a man offered her money to follow him into a field. He had not used any words about what was to happen – he had gone on talking about how a hawk had struck his chicken-run, come down as a bolt out of the blue sky, hitting up a raucous jabber of cries as it dispatched a blood-scored poult with beak and talons. He had repeated the story with minor variants, and she remembered the cow-parsley nodding its surf of umbels, the smell of ferns in the deep, green meadow. By the time his hand had travelled the length of her thigh, her head was buzzing from the monotony of his tale. The contact with her skin was a relief from his voice. It was a different form of communication, something she knew should not have been happening but which went on independent of her, as though it were being experienced by someone else, only she did not object to his eager kisses, the hirsute wrist that clumsily tore her blouse open, the stab of pain that seared her as he somehow became a part of her, forcing his different body on hers, two twisted irregularities strained into the one stem.

Marthe, who picks up clients outside the Hôtel de Ville, carries within her tormented person some of the contradictory forces that burnt out my own nerve. My inheritance of the sea is reflected in her serpentine tattoos, the intertwining, tongue-flickering snakes inked on her arms in violet, green and blue, which for her symbolise ports, sailors, the screeching of a bald monkey running amongst bollards and hawsers. All of these things had come to represent the sea passages that Marthe had never undertaken.

Marthe too had adopted her name. She knew me as Lautréamont, nothing else: a man whose interests in her were not so much sexual as vicarious – I paid to learn of other people's sexual propensities, ministers, bankers, sailors, priests, and the human link that Marthe comprised.

When I left her and returned to my attic, it was always with the fear that my room might have been broken into and my papers discovered. The other me, the youthful Ducasse, was always hiding behind the door, reproaching me for having denied him the right to live. I knew that if he could have found a way out of the captivity in which I placed him, he would have killed me.

I continued with Maldoror – his incursions into conventional states, the savagery of his attacks on absolutes, his recognition of the androgyne, the street-gangs who laid into him with boots. He could survive everything through the power afforded him by the reconciliation of opposites.

At night I would make up before the mirror but never contemplated going out. Montevideo had been a city of masks, snapdragon-coloured fireworks, the startling lipstick gash on someone of unidentifiable gender – the chance was always there in the throw of a dice, the electric jab of a firefly, that the unexpected encounter would resolve itself in a garden within the sound of the sea.

Here in the rue du Faubourg Montmartre I can feel the pressure peculiar to this age. My life has been a preparation through words for the existence I shall live when I have renounced the shield of fiction. How can they know, those casual passers-by, of the inner landscape that occupies my days? My room is piled with natural history magazines, the endless cuttings I take from English publications on birds, reptiles and batrachians. Often I have the singular vision of two eagles fighting on a high summit against a red South American sun. An amazing aerial chase is followed by the interlocking of talons, one bird forcing the other on to its back in the flailing of black pinions, until one finally goes limp, its gut eviscerated, its neck broken. It is then that I see the victor perform a weird dance to the sun, flame extending from its wing-tips, and the sun in turn growing a dark red and putting out wings over the abyss. In recognition of that great force, the eagle tears out its eyes and stands mute, head bowed before the blackening heavens.

My father's letters urge me to go south. He does this under the pretext that my fragile health would profit from the Mediterranean. But I prefer to remain here; my own apocalyptic vision is in tune with the times. A man came shouting up my stairs that the Emperor was dead, another that Paris had fallen.

A time of rumours and confusion, the great powers threatening to mobilise, and all of it means nothing to the feet treading black grapes, the hands hauling in nets and separating blue mullet and mackerel from red and green clottings of weed.

When Marthe called last night I was afraid. I had been at pains never to give her my address, but somehow she had found me out and came into my room, white-faced, black-eyed, her entire being shivering on the threshold of her nether lip. When I coaxed it out of her in my ill-humour, for my mind was locked into my work, I learnt that she had been followed for several days by a face that appeared out of the crowd with remorseless insistence but never spoke. A face that came at her without eyes and went off without looking, but seemed to know something that did not need to be seen or said. The sort of face that first occurs to you inside the head and only later materialises into an external phenomenon, confusing you as to which is which. Marthe could not explain it properly, but her occupation in life had afforded her a psychological acumen with which to assess the weird. She had witnessed almost every form of extreme behaviour, and had watched men strain towards that point where they adopt a dual nature, a persona so powerful in its desire that they momentarily tremble on the lip of transformation. But this man was not one of those who pays to dress up, be humiliated, reacquire a state of infantilism, or realise any of the more bizarre fetishes.

I gave Marthe brandy and wrapped a blanket round her; but fear was embedded in her like a snake-bite. She grew so cold that I had to bully the fire into catching and drape my black greatcoat over her. When at last she could identify things, she spoke of the man as someone who had knocked on her door late one night and to whom she had refused entry. And from that night on she felt he had never gone away. She could hear him breathing in the corridor, his shadow was huge on the stairs, his feet resounded in the street until dawn. And despite the years of selling her body indiscriminately to clients, she had remained vulnerable, vitally aware of her own physical fragility and her lack of protection from the law. This man who was like a blind pit pony wanted to trample her, rear up and annihilate her in a single blood-flash, only she wished it would come quickly and that there would be an end to terror.

For two days I sat with her, afraid of her dementia, terrified for some reason that we would be found together. I feared her death; my work was still incomplete, and I was driven by the obsession not to be distracted for a moment. But worse than that, in my distraught state I visited her room, and only later, threading back through the blue fog, did I remember that I had left her asleep in my attic. I even feared she was missing because I had killed her; but she was sitting up in bed, alert like a cat that has just woken, and biting into the black plums she had fetched from the street.

My nerves were shredded. I sat at the piano and without any notion of tune created a black thunder roll, an oppressive andante. I played with my bare nerves, breaking myself against a wall of sound as I had once opposed the rush of giant surf crashing shorewards from the blue sea-roads. I caught a sideways glance of Marthe hurriedly dressing, forcing her full breasts into black satin, desperate to be out of the room and to avoid my mood. My mind built with the bass roll, the death march towards a black sun, reached towards a visionary plane when the current subsided and sent me hurtling back to the immediate, the wineglasses I had broken, the clutter of books shelved off the piano-top, the dissonant hum swarming round the room without an exit.

Marthe had disappeared. I stood up and looked out at the dusk. A group of men were vociferating loudly in the street. Punches were thrown before an agent de police broke up the crowd, dragging the ringleader with him, a stringy bundle of a man, half starved, vehement with his party's cause.

I took out my notebook and outlined my intention to conclude *Maldoror*.

> It is my opinion that the synthetic part of my work is now complete, and what awaits me now is a concern with the analytic. Today I am going to fabricate a little novel of thirty pages; the estimated length will, in the event, remain unchanged.... I believe I have, after various attempts, at last found my definitive formula. It is the best: since it is the novel.

I knew now that the completion of my novel would be rapid, final and without interruption. I had dismissed Marthe from my life; no one ever again would have access to my person. Writing poetry involves a fictitious leap into the posthumous. The poet has to anticipate a language, a mode of thought that will intersect with the continuous future. At night I often sit and wonder at those who have written in the trust that they will be read by a pair of blue or green or grey eyes in a new century.

I go out once each day at twilight. Everything is still there – the yellow house with ivy zigzagging all over its architectural irregularities, the fish-lipped child who plays with a sailing-boat in the gutter, a dancer buying satin ballet slippers, and the red stripe of paint on the road that I have come to read as a sign, a presentiment instructing me to turn back. I have the belief that if I cross this mark my fortune will be reversed. It is as though an invisible force propels me back, and the purpose of my walk is simply to find this symbol and return. And if one day it were to go missing, so that I crossed over into an unfamiliar quarter, it is possible I should go on walking for days, powerless to halt my momentum.

When I come back indoors, I return to my writing. I bring the great beasts into abeyance on the page. I raise a whiphand to metaphor: I possess nothing but contempt for cliché. My body is periodically racked by fever, which must be the consequence of having picked up a virus on my brief return to Montevideo. In the day hours when I should be sleeping, I lie frozen, my mind lit up with visions like flares falling across waste land.

A revolution means nothing in the light of finishing my book. The frantic entreaties of one neighbour to another, shouted across balconies, to get out of the city before it is too late, leave me cold. What I see, what I read in my inner life is of a more universally cataclysmic nature. The genocidal fury of nations is nothing compared to the weird spin of the universe that comes at me slowly like a black ball I am powerless to deflect.

I take drugs to alleviate my tension. When the concierge informed me that a young woman with red hair had been round looking for me, I was so paranoid as to contemplate flight. She had left an illegible note in which I made out the words *for your own safety* before destroying it.

Even though it is summer I keep a fire burning. A rank stench streams from the gutters. There is a smell of change in the air, as though autumn has become a permanent season, as though all the autumns of the world have rolled a red fireball of leaves down the hills of Montmartre into the city. At night the old Bonapartists riot to excess before the anticipated crash occurs.

All Paris is ablaze with the scandal surrounding Prince Napoleon's murder of Victor Noir. This violent, pugnacious man fired at point-blank range through the journalist's heart, leaving the latter to crawl out into the suburban street at Auteuil and die in the gutter outside a pharmacist's. This particular murder, which went without justice, grew in my mind from the lamp-black posters to the idea that this young Jewish man, Salmon, who went under the name of Victor Noir, was in some way associated with me. I felt implicated with someone about whom I knew nothing. In my state of estrangement the murder seemed to have some association with the red paint-mark I encountered with such superstition on my daily walks. For days I was convinced that the stain on the road was really blood, and that by not informing anyone of my discovery I had contributed to Victor Noir's death. I went back to the paint-stripe and stood over it, occasionally bending to test it with a finger, and managing to work a little of the redness into my pigment, so that in some way I could identify with the murdered victim. He needed me in his dark, no matter how tenuous our thread of communication. We might have been interchangeable, only it was I who was sitting here working on the last section of *Maldoror*, my right arm lit by a late ray of sunshine probing the mist.

At night stars dust my skylight. They have become my companions in the solitary hours. On a purple night they seem closer than the lights burning in high windows. In three months my little book of poems will be published, something I wrote almost as an apologia for the shock tactics of *Maldoror*. I had to write to Darasse to raise money to pay the printer, for my father's meanness increases. He is convinced that I burn up my allowance on the night-life in Paris.

My father's advice to me in a recent letter was to disengage from a life of reckless dissolution. 'This is not the way great books come to be written. Secure yourself a career: the poet in nineteenth-century France is the fish skeleton picked up by a stray cat.'

I suppose what I fear most is that Father will have a paid agent gut my room and destroy my papers without discrimination. This is one of the reasons I so rarely go out now. And when *Maldoror* is complete, who will I be? The triumvirate of Ducasse, Lautréamont and Maldoror will have ended, and I shall be forced to adopt a new persona – a metamorphosis demanding a still further change of identity, a refurbishment of skin on the old patchy lesions.

They come more often now, those stragglers fished up out of the night's black pool – informers, occultists, thieves, political revolutionaries who have tired of every meaning except the natural silence that comes before dawn, the hour in which time seems to stand still, and the illusion of a new age is, at least for a bluish hour, a possibility.

And those who visit me, I still do not know their names. The eccentric young scholar of Gian Gastone, the last ruling Prince of the Medici family, who delights in relaying the salacities attributed to Gastone's father the Grand Duke, and how he kept a stable of boys, and how two bears were brought to dance for him in his room while he lay prostrate on a couch, cradling a wine bottle at his lips.

And another one who took part in a naturalist exploration of the Amazon and is slowly wasting away from some tropical virus which lives in his blood. He is still caught up in the river's coils, still paddling downstream through green currents into the immense silence that characterises the Brazilian forests. When he shakes, you can hear his teeth and bones rattle. His entire protection against the world is a sheath of skin so transparent that his anatomy shows through.

There are others, individual if less memorable. I have lived my life like this, associating with those who have dropped out of the social fabric. Access to this world is guarded with lions and torches. The psychotic, the insomniac, the drug addict are the modern furies who remind the conformist that man's real life involves a reversion to the primal, an inquiry into the mirror which returns his features as snake-haired, black-eyed, mouth pouring with oracular bees.

There is growing news of a war that has left me untouched. MacMahon has assembled his troops at Metz in the Rhineland, and there is news of an engagement at Saarbrücken. The

Empress is left as Regent at St Cloud. Some say the Emperor is too ill to be lifted on to his horse, and the signs are painted for revolution in his absence. I try to pretend that what is happening is not real, that it will go away if only I lose myself in the discoveries of inner space. For the last three nights I have had no callers: the streets are unsafe. Not even a night-wolf would quarter the terrorists who batter a jeweller's display to a lake of twinkling shards. Grubby fists close over emerald brooches, diamond aigrettes – street girls are paid in sapphires by the coarse and indiscriminate.

Some months ago I wrote: 'Those men who have resolved to detest their fellow-beings have forgotten that one must start by detesting oneself.' This is the premise for all moral behaviour. Self-detestation establishes a balance whereby humility acquires a degree of greatness. What I see, what I say, what I do, each is an attempt to reconcile my approximate self with a higher being, the overself. That I fall short is part of the latter's greatness and not a condition of my own weakness.

I have begun to envisage barricading myself in. This race against time, the writing hand trying to outclock the big hand of eternity, leads to mistrust of the body, suspicion of the mind, a realisation of the incompleteness of human endeavour. I can remember in my childhood waking to the shriek of those killed under Rosas. My recurrent nightmare was that of a man standing at the foot of the bed and opening out his hands to reveal a heart that was still beating. My mother would be woken by my screams, and her protective warmth and the camomile tea she prepared became a ritual associated with the night.

I could doubtless bundle up my papers and possessions and leave Paris – head south and restore my health in a blue climate. But I have resolved to stay until the house is fired. The faces of revolutionaries resemble those monsters with which I have peopled *Maldoror* – the giant crab, the female shark, the octopus, all of them scavengers for offal, predators when on the offensive. One could not have imagined that Paris harbours so many defectors, people who seem to have been waiting half a lifetime in doorways, alleys, courtyards to intersect with the current revolution.

Rumour has it that the Empress holds court in black and wears a jet diadem – the lights are on all night in the Tuileries as the last of her ministers feverishly plot a means of resistance. Paris has become a city of insomniacs, its night fever throbs through my arteries. I could see a crowd of men dancing on a roof, throwing a girl up into the air and catching her, before the building began to crack with crazy blue and green flames.

Last night they tried my door but moved on. When I went out in the morning the red paint-mark had disappeared. Part of the road had been broken up and barricaded. It is a sign that I am without boundaries and alone.

The Eye 8

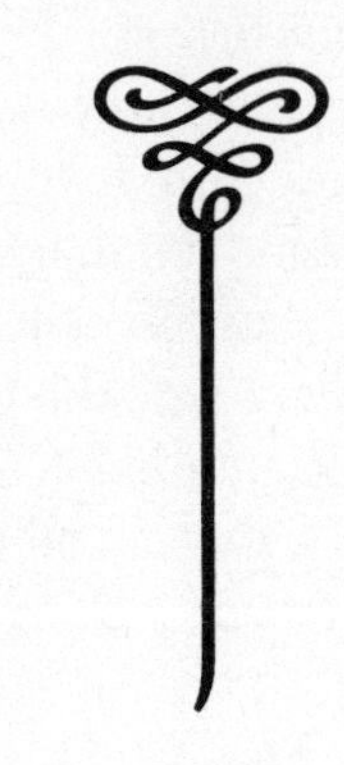

The situation in Paris grows progressively worse. There is little chance of my communication reaching you before the city capitulates to revolution. I have risked my life in staying on and shall leave once I have dispatched this final report.

Isidore Ducasse, or rather the person I assumed to be your son, has a double. The regular visitors to his room are by now well known to me – the vagrants, those who appear to have no identity during the day hours – but this person without any doubt answers to your son's description. Having ascertained that Isidore Ducasse remained behind in his room, I succeeded in following this double as far as the rue de Rivoli, where he finally disappeared down an alley without trace. He may have got wind of my following him and hidden in a basement.

The possibility alarms me. It occurs to me that I may at times have been tracking the wrong person. This young man also walks with a stoop, is unshaven, has long, unkempt hair like your son, and dresses in identical clothes – a black suit, white shirt and red bow. I tell myself that I am wrong, but the facts are indisputably there. I have witnessed the two of them on three separate occasions. They link arms in the street, discourse ear to ear and are generally inseparable when together.

It occurs to me that my course of investigation belongs as I see it almost exclusively to one and not the other. But to which one? It seems too improbable to suggest that your son has a double who serves as a decoy. Where would he find such a person?

It is true that fear, insufficient food – we are now in a state of rationing – and bacterial water can all contribute to a state of disturbance; but the phenomena I describe are not the result of a deranged mind.

I gained access to Isidore Ducasse's room yesterday by means of bribing the concierge. The room is stripped to a state of basic necessities. He appears to have packed up his personal belongings in expectation of leaving. The concierge hardly sees him. She complains only of his playing the piano at night despite repeated requests not to do so. He pays her a quarter in advance, which may account for her conviction that your son has most certainly not vacated his room. His double appears to live in an hotel in the rue Vivienne.

In the course of my life I have been called on to examine a great number of rooms, but few have left so deep an impression on me. This has nothing to do with the furnishings – there is nothing untoward in his place. It has more to do with an atmosphere. The room emits a sense of violent disturbance – it is both too silent and too charged. Whatever goes on there will make it hard for a future tenant.

Circumstances make it inadvisable for me to remain in Paris. It is possible that your son has already gone, but I saw one or the other of the two out in the street yesterday....

Chapter 8

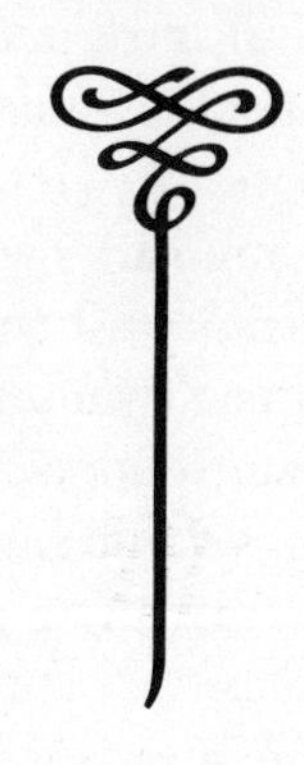

Dying begins with an anomaly of smell. It is no more than a catch in the air, an essence that was never separated from breathing, but is suddenly detectable as a scent. It is the closest we ever come to realising the self as something tangible. For twenty-four years that secretion has escaped my olfactory attention. I could imagine it taking the form of a white butterfly settling on a black pansy.

I am systematically destroying everything that is not vitally necessary to my existence. Letters, books, clothes, journals, the few possessions belonging to my mother that I brought with me from Montevideo, and all of the correspondence I have received while in Paris. If they take me, they will have to name me, and that is no easy matter.

If I look for certainty now it is in the mirror. I approach it like a fish, believing that I could without the least resistance swim through the glass and find myself on the other side looking out at the fictional characters I have created. These are the real people who will guide me into that dimension where the imagination is reality.

What I am physically, flesh and blood, has a cheap price on it. The streets are full of the dead, organically externalised like the contents of a slaughterhouse. I have to resist the attraction to carnage that preoccupied my early youth. Whatever it was I tried to realise in the interaction between extreme fear in an animal and the butchered quiet that came as an aftermath to that instinctive panic, has remained unresolved.

There is no way out. Travel and mail have come to a halt. I could arrange to leave Paris by night – my way of life has put me into contact with friends who could effect that, but affairs are thrown into confusion by news that MacMahon's army, disgraced in its campaign, is now retreating on the capital with a view to saving the Empire. It is extraordinary how in the world of external reality whole nations will rise for an idea conceived by a cripple, a syphilitic tyrant, a mad boy-king playing with skulls instead of toys, the pride of a man who, to reinstate his own slighted dignity, will churn a field into blood, leave a wick of smoke in place of a corn harvest and return victorious to his sycophants.

Poetry has gone underground. It has disappeared like the goddess to join the king of the underworld, the patron of darkness, of shadow-men who leave no imprint on the asphodels. I am responsible for the lives I have created; they draw closer, cold-water denizens in their imaginal fish-glitter, alive at a temperature that is too zeroic for humans to reach, lunar cold, mineral, planetary in its blue cool.

'A meadow, three rhinoceroses, half a catafalque, these are descriptions. They can be memory or prophecy. They are not the paragraph I am on the point of completing.'

The variations are endless. A blue river, a red parasol open in a white dinghy at Valvins, a black marble tomb covered with carnations. Where I conclude the sentence is arbitrary. It arrests the limitless possibilities arising from a group of images that could be reorganised in any number of permutations.

They will say I ended in the madhouse and that my novel is molten lava; crazy, black, devouring. Imaginative involvement does this – it demands that the author follows his own downward slide rather than steps aside to direct his work independent of his being.

If I were in Montevideo now I should be within reach of the surf. It would not cure me, but its protective, insulating wall of sound would lift me up above its smash-line into clear, dazzling light. In Paris that wash hits my window only when it snows, or when a bright shower falls from a luminous April sky.

Occasionally medical orderlies dressed in white smocks with red crosses on their arms, and carrying stretchers, hurry towards the sound of an explosion. As yet, the insurrection is contained. It is my own head that has the city spin like a cone of fire. I seldom eat. When I drink red wine my mind swims in an alcoholic sea like a crimson fish.

I have this notion as I huddle here in a blanket that it is Isidore Ducasse who will die and not the Comte de Lautréamont. It is he who was always suspect – Isidore who never detached himself from his mother, and who was last seen riding bareback across the grasslands outside Montevideo. Only I shall not be there to live on as Lautréamont, the autonomous satellite who has sat at the piano, the writing-desk, and created a life for Maldoror. Fictions live like paper tigers, the resonant come alive in red and black flame when the right generation decants blood on to the page.

I could invent a death for myself: the narrative of a person without an identity – a death so far removed from the ways in which we envisage our end that it would alter the concept of dying. But I insist it is a fiction, for that is the closest we come to reality.

My invented death suggests a fabricated life, but that is for you the reader to decide. My only awareness is now, in the ultraviolet leads extending into the unconscious, and in the infra-red slow exposures of consciousness. To divert you, I have suggested a death that may or may not be plausible – how it occurs is dependent on the potential of language to falsify.

It begins with a concertina effect. A gable collapses at night, its dull slow-motion attempt to remain horizontal in the air is only a momentary thing before the accelerative process brings it down flat. You are asleep at the time and mistake it for surf blasting across a shingled gradient. You may be one surface lower, dreaming again that you are an aquatic egg in the womb and that a shock to your mother's system has registered in a cataclysmic way. The hum is terrible – it sets up a vibration that almost discharges you. But the volume of sound stays. You try to associate it with a dream falling back like a wreck into the vortex, only it will not disperse in depth, taking you down with it, but remains in the air, intransigent, building to a consistency that seems trapped at roof-top level, before you stumble awake to find the red flare already pointing its flames skywards. It is nearer this time. A street away, and it must be the tobacconist's shop with the proprietor's apartment above, which is lit. This little man, with his Polish descent and dusty black suit, has a printing press in the cellar. He used to publish pornography – algolagnic books with explicit lithographs depicting young girls being disciplined with pliant canes. Their dishevelled froth of petticoats revealed the black stockings and garters that were clearly his obsession. Had he got clear of the flames, or did the smoke catch him asleep, so that he never saw the blankets crumple with fire?

The conflagration is a factual incident in my drift towards a union with my imagined subjects. What there is of *Maldoror* – six cantos which encapsulate an imaginary universe – is now so much printer's ink and paper. Whatever copies exist will be destroyed by the city's blaze.

Things keep coming back to me. My father's repressed limp, the sparkling granulations of my mother's face-powder, the violet crescent under Monsieur Flammarion's left eye, and the stiletto, sheathed low down on the ankle as I had first observed it in my confrontation with the Queen of Hearts. And who were the real men? Those who lived on inside my head, isolated by a particular that impressed the memory cells, or those living organisms pursuing their day in the immediate present, unconscious of my imposing a drag on things they had forgotten, caught up in new planes of experience as they stepped out of a portico under limes into bright sunlight?

I try to convince myself that there is a way of disappearing which is more like life than death. If we could maintain the narrative we might get through with a referential schema of things, like a man who has crossed a stream and placed his wet footprints on the sandy bank. There would be something, no matter how little, to go on – a right foot, a left, another pronounced right, a less defined left, and then a petering out. But those few blotched steps would be sufficient to serve as a guide to memory. From those alone one could rethink one's life, dream it again so that the sharp angles became blurred, and what remained was a silvering, like the unreal light in childhood when we wake too early and a blackbird sings in the apple tree, and for a brief moment its song is our only claim on consciousness.

In between the intervals of noise there are periods of quiet. Since I have begun to compose with my mind, committing nothing to paper in my bare room, I have evolved a new method of composition, one that demands committing visual flashes to memory. Storing them as a brain camera might.

This is my conception of a future novel, one which resonates inwardly, builds up a series of inner pictures, and continues once I am on the other side of the light.

I have begun to compose a dialogue with my shadow. He and I are living independent of the troops, the siege, the accelerated footsteps in the street. My system compensates for my inability to play the piano. I spend my time composing the narrative of an impossible death.

He had conceived of death as constellated in the future. To get there would require a journey. It was the presence of a bluebottle in the room, ink-stained and squat in a sunbeam, the gauze wings vibrating involuntarily, that convinced him death was closer than the blue pulsation he was observing, for it was inside him and required no journey to reach. And had he not already experienced a death? Was he not an impostor who had repressed and subverted another's life, and should he not have learnt from the other's death? It was Isidore Ducasse who argued with him in the blue sunbeams; it was he who by some malign dispensation demanded recompense for never having lived. Lautréamont was running out of power. The fever must have been on him for a long time, for when he tried to get up he had the sensation of being composed of light. He could fly around the room if only he allowed himself to levitate. It was easy. The ceiling was as reachable as the floor – it required just the slightest push to get there and rest, looking down on the dishevelled bed.

Someone must have come into the room, for a bowl of soup had been placed on the bedside table. His first thought was to search for the pages he had written, a reflex action that had his hands feel under the bed before he remembered his new method of committing everything to memory. In his mind he saw himself reclaiming his pictorial narrative; restoring it to an ordered sequence, then taking it apart again and magnifying it into incongruously juxtaposed images.

There was somebody else in the room. He must have come in out of the November air, for there was a scent of cold fog and smoke on his clothes, that smell a cat brings in from the night of grasses, damp leaves, a barn's mildewed beams. The young man was unnaturally tall and stooped, his green eyes showed from beneath straw-blond hair which he was in the habit of pushing out of his eyes. He was nervous, hesitant, someone who had come here for a particular purpose. He stood in front of the oval mirror in which I used to conduct shadow-plays and checked his appearance. I watched his image steady and undergo a cooling process. It settled into its reflection as ice fits the contours of a pond. The face was deliberating something, for its expression was grave, profound, deliberate in killing an equivocal concept, and finally resolved in its intention. I noticed the immaculate choice of clothes: the white blouse, the black suit, the soft boots unmarked by the street, the very things I should have chosen. His movements denoted both challenge and fear. He went to the window as though he were long familiar with the view over the city, and propped himself up on his elbows, staring out at the winter panorama. He must have done this often during the years I had lived here, for his movements suggested a perfect knowledge of the room, an intimacy with space, a calculation of footsteps that were accustomed to the proportions of the room. This man had been careful with his hands; their only flaw was a rose-thorn of royal-blue ink ingrained on the right index finger. For a moment I imagined he had come to interrogate me about the manuscript. Who was this insane Maldoror? And what was the extent of his perverse crimes against humanity? I could hear the proposed questions rapped out in a mute but lethal staccato. He would establish my guilt as a propagator of psychological upheaval on a universal scale. I had dared to anticipate the future – my imagination had smoked the bees out of their hive, set them irascibly buzzing in a malevolent black string. It was obvious that the young man was an informer, an interpreter, a member of the military police. He would manifest an implacable patience, a mathematical coldness in his determining, an unshakeable belief that I would concede to his condemnation of my work as inspired by madness.

He continued to stare out of the window. The violet dusk had deepened to a blue-black density. One watery star became two before there was the sound of rain settling in – a brisk tapping on the skylight, a hurried punctuation of crystals sparkling on glass. For an instant I was back in my father's house, inhaling the aphrodisiac sea-breeze and listening to Alma close the white shutters at nightfall. Correspondingly I was in flight across a beach, running to outpace the stooped young man whose features had grown into the more refined facial characteristics of the person who was treating my attic with the familiarity of home.

I was startled. He had taken off his tight-fitting black jacket and stood there in a white blouse. He was untying his red bow, stringing the creases out of it and twisting it into a noose. His eyes met mine once and hammered their concentration like rivets into the back of my mind. One of my last visitors had mentioned seeing a young man hanged from a lamppost by the mob. They had rouged his cheeks and painted his mouth before stringing him up. All day they had toyed with him like a puppet, pushing the body backwards and forwards like a child's swing, or letting it oscillate from side to side. The mob had been too congested to disperse; they crowded in like a jackal pack hungry to strip the flesh from the bone.

When I looked again his breath and eyes were on my face, narrowing in an indefinite suspension. Something was pressing down on me. I had the illusion that I was under water and fighting the apprehension of falling asleep before I could break the surface with the force of my head. It was a long way down, a searing spiral – pane after pane of water shattered into exploding prisms. I saw the pages of my book unleaf into an aquatic storm, the ink remaining unsmudged despite their immersion. They were forming a paper-dance, a choreographed tilting of pages into a symmetrical geometry, now a pyramidal formation, now a pentagram, a hexagon, the attenuated figure of a dancer suddenly snapping tight into the rectangle of a book.

The tighter the constriction, the more relaxed I grew. I was headed somewhere my intruder could not follow. Light was flooding in, a sense of fluid mobility, a luminous core pulsating with the radial energy of the sun. I was already beyond pain before his hands relaxed their grip. I watched him from the vantage-point of the ceiling put on his jacket, hurry down the stairs and escape into the insurgent mob who were invading the street.